D0230280

BRIGHT
AIR
BLACK

ALSO BY DAVID VANN

Fiction

Aquarium
Goat Mountain
Dirt
Caribou Island
Legend of a Suicide

Non-fiction

Last Day on Earth: A Portrait of the NIU School Shooter
A Mile Down: The True Story of a Disastrous Career at Sea

BRIGHT
AIR
BLACK

DAVID
VANN

WILLIAM HEINEMANN: LONDON

1 3 5 7 9 10 8 6 4 2

William Heinemann
20 Vauxhall Bridge Road
London SW1V 2SA

William Heinemann is part of the Penguin Random House group of companies
whose addresses can be found at global.penguinrandomhouse.com.

Copyright © David Vann 2017

David Vann has asserted his right to be identified as the author of this Work in
accordance with the Copyright, Designs and Patents Act 1988.

First published in Great Britain by William Heinemann in 2017
(First published in the United States of America by Black Cat,
an imprint of Grove Atlantic, in 2017)

www.penguin.co.uk

A CIP catalogue record for this book is available from the British Library.

ISBN 9780434023349

Printed and bound by Clays Ltd, St Ives plc

Penguin Random House is committed to a sustainable future
for our business, our readers and our planet. This book is made from
Forest Stewardship Council® certified paper.

Medea bade them land and propitiate Hecate with sacrifice. Now all that the maiden prepared for offering the sacrifice may no man know, and may my soul not urge me to sing thereof. Awe restrains my lips.

—*The Argonautica*, Apollonius (translation R. C. Seaton)

What mortals hope, the gods frustrate.
From our dull lives and loves they make
an unexpected passion play.
They turn the bright air black . . .

—*Medea*, Euripides (translation Robin Robertson)

Author's Note

I was lucky to be the captain of an ancient Egyptian sailing ship, a reconstruction with archaeologist Cheryl Ward for a French film that airs periodically on NOVA, titled *Building Pharaoh's Ship*. I was there for the construction, designed the rigging, and sailed it in the Red Sea, recreating voyages to the Land of Punt during Hatshepsut's reign 3,500 years ago. That type of Egyptian ship is what the Argo most likely would have been, so I described my own experiences as I wrote this voyage of the Argonauts with Jason and Medea. I also sailed my own boat through all the Greek islands, beginning in Croatia and ending in Turkey, to visit Korinth and many other archaeological sites. Unlike Euripides' *Medea*, which is set in his time 800 years later, *Bright Air Black* is set during Medea's time, 3,250 years ago, following the archaeological evidence and never straying from realism (there are no centaurs or chariots rising into the air). The time period is what the Greeks considered the beginning, but it's really the end of an older world, the fall of the Bronze Age, and *Medea* is a leftover, a threat from this earlier time.

Her father a golden face in darkness. Appearing in torch-light over the water and vanishing again. Face of the sun, descendant of the sun. Betrayal and rage. Four plumes along his mask, a scattering of light, a kind of mane. His shield of many hides a hollowed blackness. Ashen spear a thin line, then gone. The sail above him bowed like the belly of an ox grown large as a god, hooves making no sound in the water below.

Nothing will stop him, Medea knows. He has lost too much. All she can do is slow him. She reaches down for a piece of her brother, a forearm strong and strangely soft now, already cooling, and drops it into the sea, almost without sound, buried by the splash of oars.

She has done this for Jason and will do more, she knows. Her brother dismembered at her feet. This is how the world begins.

Dark wood in darker water, a sea of ink, and pattern felt but unseen, quartering waves caught only in glimpses. Wood thick beneath them, lines creaking. Thick ropes of the steering at her back, groaning under pressure from the rudders. With every small wave she rises and falls and twists, and Jason and his men repeat every movement a moment later. All held together as one, barbarian and her Minyae. Each hull a home.

Flesh that should sink but will not, a forearm too small to notice in torchlight in that darkness but seen nonetheless. Her father commanding the sail lowered, the oars shipped. Great ox belly deflating, no longer holding light, gone dark and rumpled, the upper yard coming down. Oar faces in a row high over the water catching light and winking out again, the ship coming about. The hull dark, unseen, her father standing above. Bending now and reaching for his son.

A howl she would hear even from another sea, matched inside her, and if she could go back, she would.

Her father's ship drifts. Lost and receding, torches shrinking, drawing closer together. Jason's men pulling at the oars, practiced thieves. No talk among them. Watching her. No light, no sound except oar and sail and rope. A heavy breath of them, a heat.

Medea is without words, without thought. She has unstrung the world, pulled some vital thread and unraveled all. Nothing to do now but hold her breath and find out whether a new world re-forms. Her task is to portion carefully, use the pieces of her brother sparingly.

Her father raises his sail again, smaller now. Golden mask a fainter torch, spear and shield gone. Oars working invisible, glints of water disrupted and nothing more. But she knows his will. These Minyae no match.

Her father would pull the sun into its place and pull it down again, do his father's work. Bronze and fire and gold, all forms of the sun. Endless rage, and no reason, no stopping, the burning away of all. Her father descended from this, and she too. Demigods. Humans beyond human law.

By his decree, men buried not in the ground but in the air, strung from trees in untanned ox hides. Twisting forever above, the women below. He would balance earth and air. He believes he can do that. His rage now a simple disbelief that any of this could happen and to him. All of it foretold, but he didn't think to fear his daughters, feared only his son. Men visible, hung and rotting in their sacks and remembered, women invisible below.

Already he's drawing closer. Medea clings to the bulwark and sternpost and fears tumbling over the side, as if what she has done could claim her at any moment, pull her into black water. Kneeling in her brother, wet against her thighs. Smell of blood and viscera, sacrifice. A smell she's known all her life. To Helios the sun, and to other gods, to Hekate. Jason an able witch, slitting a lamb's throat to Hekate, burning a pyre, inviting serpents to writhe in the oaks above and hellhounds to howl, walking away with the strength to not look back. Her own strength failing. Kneeling in her brother's remains too much.

Lurch of each wave a sideways push, her face over water, hull falling away, caving. She can almost wish for this, to slip beneath the surface, cold and airless, silent, without motion except a gradual fall. All the world gone, the sun mute. A place even her father would not reach her.

Hekate, dark one, make this darkness last. Medea speaks in a tongue no man on the Argo can understand. Widen this sea and let this blood that drips from our decks thicken and slow my father. Blood of the sun. My own blood, my own brother. I give you this.

Medea can see the waters coagulate and bind, waves slow and flatten, wind lose its hold, her father mired by what came from his own veins. The sun held below the surface of the sea, swallowed and never rebirthed. Held by Nute, blue god of the Egyptians, ancient god, ancient woman, older than the sun. Helios swallowed each night and sailing through the pathways of Nute's body toward birth but tricked this time by vanity. The sun wanting human form, wanting descendants and generations to worship. That blood now made into an anchor, the pathways become endless, and no light.

Medea the one who would end a god and all his descendants and the day-lit world. She would do this. She knows this is true, that whatever binds other people to each other has no hold on her. She is bound only by elements, by water and air and earth and fire and blood. She will do what her father will not and what Jason will not. She should be queen with no king, a Hatshepsut.

Where the Argo might take her. Iolcus, Jason's home, but who can say where else? Egypt, birthplace of the older gods, an older world. All ships drawn there to see the long echo of time.

But first they must outrun her father. It will be light soon, and nowhere to hide on this long open coast.

Jason, she calls. And when he comes, she turns away from her father, lies back in the remains of her brother, all the Argonauts watching. Skin lit by torchlight from far over the water, wandering, a luminescence that might originate in him or be only imagined. Eyes depthless, lit and black again. But his urgency is real, his heat. She pulls him close, binds him, mining his breath and heart. All else has been lost. This is what she has now. She will master this.

Night prolonged, Hekate hearing. Medea no longer a maiden, her blood mixed with her brother's and dripping into the sea. She understands now that her father must be broken, every last part of him broken, all taken away, that the prophecy was about this, about the humbling of a king. Medea the destroyer of kings. She would have a world without them.

Her Minyae so proud of their golden fleece, a theft ordered by another king, Pelias, in Iolcus. But there are hundreds of golden fleeces, untanned hides sifting the heavy dust of gold from every mountain stream that feeds into the great valley of her home. Hung from trees to dry before the gold is beaten and shaken from them. Something witnessed and taken far away and told and retold until there was only one fleece, made itself of gold, and to take it is to take a king's power.

Jason has hung it now from the lower yard, beneath the sail, and believes the ship will be faster. But his men will find gold dust on their shoulders and backs and will begin to find their outlines in starlight, and by the time they've reached Iolcus, the fleece will be only a sheep's hide, with no gold left in it at all.

Her father is gaining. Medea would have her oarsmen transformed, that fine dusting of gold, and she would have their oars ply air, the ship lift and sail free of water. She can feel the weight of the boat, pressing down into the sea, burying itself, a kind of grave, slowing. Her father's sail lit by torch against black, straining closer, eager, following a track invisible and inevitable through veins of night. Cave journey, unseen walls. Quiet. The sea could be tilted downward and they wouldn't know.

Medea clings to the stern and fears. She must drop another piece of her brother into the water, but she can't be too early or too late. Too early and there won't be enough of him to last. Too late and her father might not stop, might overtake and return for the remains.

Spear tips in the light, fifty cold metal slits glinting and disappearing and appearing again. She can see the curve of backs, her father's men rowing. Their spears hugged close, ready. They've gone to war before. Their sail pulls at the mast, pinned above and below on its yards. Close enough now to hear the lower binding creak, close enough to see a man standing aft with his legs braced, holding a line thick as his arm to tug at a lower edge, to find the wind. Ponderous heaving of the sail, restless and bloated. Her father knows this sea better than the Minyae, knows the wind rises now just before morning. His helmsmen know not to work the rudders, know to let the boat slide free and gain momentum. The rudders beside Medea working too much, snaking back and forth, turned against each other, losing power and speed. These helmsmen afraid.

She can see her father's hand on his spear.

I let him have me, she yells to her father over the water. Here on deck, in front of his sailors. The daughter of a king. Or what used to be a king.

She sees his spear and shield brought in closer.

In every land, we'll show the fleece, and I'll say it's the only one. The robe of a king, and no king without it.

He raises his spear, pulls back and lunges with a roar. Thin line in that night, arcing, glint of light, starfall, and no way of knowing where the arc will end. But Medea opens her arms wide, makes herself as big a target as she can be, and laughs as the spear falls short, faint rip into water and gone.

I'll save my brother's heart and say it's yours. I'll say the king of Colchis is dead and any may have his land. I'll hold your dried little heart and pretend to weep and say I loved my father but he was too weak.

Her father too proud to say anything in return. Silent behind his mask. Made smaller.

Descendant of the sun, she yells. If this is true, show yourself. All is being taken. Impotent king. No king.

Medea takes a piece of her brother, a thigh, heavy and tough, muscled, and licks blood from it, dark and thick. She spits, licks and spits again and again, three times to atone. Mouth filled with the taste of her family's blood, and she throws this piece of Helios into the waves.

She has ripped out all their hearts, she knows. Her father's crew crippled to see him made smaller. She will humble him until there's nothing left, until his men don't know why they're rowing. They will collect the pieces of the son and wonder that demigods can fall so easily.

A cry from her father, anguish at the sight of another piece, and he turns away to command the sail lowered. Men gather at the stern to let down the upper yard and collapse all power. A ship without wind no more than a collection of sticks. Oars held out of the water, wooden insect with thirty legs, coming about, stalling. Her father bent over the side, reaching for his son but missing. The boat rolling though the seas are small. Long wooden yards of the fallen sail tipping down almost to the water, then rising into the sky.

Her father bellowing in grief, strange sound like some animal in the field. Pushing back through his oarsmen to reach his son from the stern. No pretending to be a king. Only a father. The air in Medea's lungs gone heavy. Her father falling away into the night and she can't see whether he recovers the piece, his boat turned and blocking her view.

Her brother gone. She misses him there, far away, in his father's arms, and yet most of him is here. She kneels in him still. Impossible to locate the dead. Her brother everywhere and nowhere, and everything she's felt for him remains. No part of him dies when he's gone. He's only gone.

Argonauts pulling hard at the oars, sail full. She is with strangers. They feel nothing for her brother. And if Jason feels nothing for her brother, what can he feel for her?

Her father's ship receding, fading into night, torchlights narrowing, rotating, and so they must be circling back for her brother's thigh. Heavy piece of flesh, perhaps too heavy to pull easily from the waves. And now it could be lost in that darkness. They'll have to search, and they can't know where they've been. The ship drifting in the wind, but the wind with no hold on mostly submerged flesh, hidden, bobbing just at the surface, a whiteness in the black. With every moment more lost and her father more desperate. A future he could never have seen. A king always at the center, never without reference.

Hekate, keep this night, Medea says. Let it stay a while longer. Nute, do not give birth yet.

For her father, the sea is growing and his boat spinning. He tells his helmsmen one direction and then another, every patch of water black and unfamiliar and the same. The wind rising and waves larger. He could be fifty boat lengths now from his son, or only an arm's length and still not see. He should know when his own flesh is near. There should be something that binds.

Medea sails farther away with the rest of her brother, but what she feels is a need to help her father. Be his eyes in that night, take his arm and guide him. Put her brother back together and breathe life into him again. Call on Hekate to re-form a body and sacrifice her own. Make her family whole even if she is lost. Overwhelming feeling, an anchor in her chest, lodged and pulling, her body being torn apart, and this is how women are formed. Slaves. But she will not be a slave. She will feel this need to help her father and she will not help him. She will grieve her brother and kneel in his remains and throw the next piece overboard when the time comes. She will not be mastered. If it is natural to be a slave, she will be unnatural.

Water in a seam at the stern, luminescent. Curling from both sides, folding inward, then spinning off into miniature whorls filled with stars. No moon, no torches, but the sea with its own light, the heavens submerged and flung and still burning. Whatever made Helios himself, repeated here in fragment.

Medea has never seen this world before, never would have guessed its existence. Her first voyage on the sea. Any shape can be found in the sky below. Great aquarian bulls charging, the most fanciful birds with tail feathers reaching, slim, without end. Even her father, a gathering of stars with plumes like his mask, and the weight of darkness attached, rotating slowly and pulling all toward him. More life even than fire. Hekate found in fire, in sparks and sheets of flame, but unlimited here. No distraction of ground or wind, not limited to the fuel of wood but freed and infinite and transparent, able to reveal all. A landscape as unknown and unbound as the felt landscape within, seen by every man who has gone to sea at night for war or fishing but never shared. No man has told Medea of this. And what are these stars? Where did they come from?

New world, or an opening of the old. She can't find the constellations, familiar forms. Looking into the stars below, she might even find a new god, as the first gods were found by looking into the sky. A god is whatever can't be reached.

None of these stars fixed. Flung in orbits by the passing of Medea and her crew, a more responsive sky, what she's always wanted the heavens to be, not cold and distant.

Medea wants to return to the first naming, to when the sky above was as responsive as this one below, before it cooled and hardened and was known. She would have begun with a woman pregnant, Nute covering all, and she would have wandered through every land for years learning the shape of that woman, careful not to draw lines, letting the stars shift for as long as they needed, and only then would she have named the lesser constellations, the head and breasts and feet and hands and womb of this woman, each with its own attributes and promise, shape of all that is needed for worship in life below. And then smaller constellations still for each story, for each myth. She would be there to shape what is wrong and what is right. And then she would push every human head down into the sea, make them forget the sky and every myth and burn their eyes with endlessly shifting pattern in which new gods and their myths are born and die every moment.

What myth can hold when you kneel in your brother's remains? When you slit his throat yourself? What story can guide us if we can betray all?

Dark one, Medea says to the water. Let everything that binds fall. Let all that is known be confused. Let all that we are die. Let me be most hated of all women, and most true.

Endless night, but the sailors make no comment, if they even notice. Go about their business. Thieves with pygmy hearts. They've lost nothing.

The largest wears the hide of a bear and walks toward Medea, loosening the cloth around his hips. Jason giving her up so soon. But this bear-man stops at the rudder posts, holds onto one and leans back over the water, shits into the sea, fouling the air. The breeze not strong enough, and now the other men feel free to do the same.

This is the sea burial of a prince, she says in their language, waving with her arm for them to stay away. A future king of Colchis. She sees one grinning, teeth in starlight. A game to them. Jason unconcerned. He takes his turn at the oars, as vacant and stone eyed as the rest.

They drink water from clay vessels foreign to her, eat food taken from her home. Sounds of chewing on lamb that was grilled over her father's fires. Sweet smell of honey to mix with the smells of shit and viscera.

Hekate's hold loosening, the first deep blue appearing over the mountains that rim her home. Jagged outlines of black, and the stars fading. She looks down again into the water and is losing this world, too, the surface thickening, becoming opaque even in this first shadow of light.

Her grandfather climbing the other side of the world. Holding the reins, hooves pounding air. She used to wait for him at this hour when she was a girl, waking before the rest, hoping to see him. The beginning, perhaps, of her interest in night, unintended. Descended from the sun and worshipping darkness. Who she is makes no sense to her. How she became. What she will become still.

The other side of the world steep and nearly endless. Long climb in that chariot, light appearing long before he clears the peaks. A place where mountains wear away, long slides of loose stone, without trees, directionless. Any other god would become lost. She feels this place inside her now, barren heart, no living or growing thing. She waits for Jason to notice her, his face only one of nearly fifty pale dark-blue shields in this light, rolling away with each heave at the oars then returning.

All these men belong, all act as one, the rowers, the men who stand before her working the rudders, the men holding thick lines that guide the sail, even those who have stopped to eat or drink and sit low on the deck. They've fallen into a wordless routine, their minds blank.

Jason, she calls. She can't wait for him to notice.

He pauses, the other faces rolling away from him and returning and heaving away again. He lowers the handle of his oar to the deck and comes aft to kneel beneath the rudder posts. His hair in curls. Nose fine and straight, lips full, but his beauty in the soft curve of his cheeks, the smooth fall away from that nose, an open plain beneath each eye. She pulls him close with both hands and presses her lips to this soft place, feels the blink of his lashes, his thick hair in her hands.

He doesn't move, his breath caught, and she smiles, presses her lips to the other cheek. You are mine, she says in a tongue he won't understand. By the old stars above and the new stars below, I will rule your heart. You are the land I conquer.

This ship riding a thin plain between two heavens, and she would turn it over, make the underworld the air they breathe, wet stars bumping against Jason's broad back and flung away in the wake. She'll find shelter here. She curls in closer to his chest and he wraps his arms around. Damp with sweat, on fire from the oars, smell of him and heavy beating of blood. His sides flared out in ridges, thick and rounded. She holds these in her hands, bulwarks to keep her from falling overboard. The night heavy and warm, another sea, and she closes her eyes, longs to sleep, exhausted, but he pries her away, leaves her kneeling, returns to his oar.

As if the rowing were saving them. These pieces of her brother are saving them. Her father would be on their decks now, hacking through flesh in his rage until no part matched any other, until no Minyan hero could be assembled by his kin for funeral rites, until they'd have to be burned together in a great pile. Only Medea is saving them, only her sacrifice.

She turns away, sees the mountains of her home shadow teeth now against a paler blue, the light she would live in always, the sun held on the far slope, offering enough only for outline and texture, all softened and cooled. The sea a color she's never seen, not the same as a river or pond, not the same as viewed from land. Deeper, darker, a melted hue and shadows everywhere, interrupted light, broken, each hollow something you could reach into and never find bottom. Her first sunrise from the sea, and why did she have to wait this long? It was here, not far away, every morning of her life.

She realizes only too late that she'll never see the light rise behind these mountains again, that she's missed seeing them transform in the light, that she's looked too long at the water and lost her home. Already the ridges and peaks are edged in white, losing substance and depth. All is being flattened and won't return again.

Her grandfather would erase all. White glare each morning an oblivion. Distance gone. Shape and shadow and being. Eyes without use, and this water an open desert with no refuge.

Forest at the edge of her home, original forest, wet with mist, rising steeply, mountain after mountain without end. No flattening of distance but each fold expanding, each ravine become larger. Moss and fern. Gnarled old roots black and intertwined. Needles dense above, branches twisted and the tops gone from sight. Places even her grandfather can't reach. Deadfall and dark rock, caves in those mountains and the forest itself a cave. Her home. In that stillness, walking beneath those trees. Cold breath, all sound muted, always watched and alone, a place on the edge of panic, as if the forest might swallow or she could be hunted. Wolf and bear. And the overwhelming sense of being alive, the thud of a heart beating. A strange freedom not given to girls, but one she took anyway, walking out alone at night even when she was very young. A home she always knew was hers, antidote to the sun, escape from her father, a place instead of a mother. A refuge she can't imagine herself without, lost and gone now, and she knows she'll never return, that she's made herself an outcast and will be a stranger even to herself. Why she did this, she doesn't know. Love the erasure of everything else, a blinding worse even than the sun.

Madness without thought. One act and then another, inevitable, unstoppable, never questioned. He appeared from nowhere, came out of the fog at the edge of the city. Strange fog for this season, late burning, and so he and his men were able to anchor in the river and walk through groves where the dead hung in their ox hides and come right to her home unchallenged. Jason stood before her, unlikely, something she could not have imagined. A half-god, favored, a gift. Given to her, gazing at her. And from that first moment, all was set in motion. All subversion of her father's plans, the many ways she would help Jason and his men, all as if it were already accomplished. Not fate, but something waiting inside her. Fate no more than a brute plow dragged along, but this was something wanted, sprung from desire unknown and released, a recognition. The closest Medea has ever known to truth. The most certain moment of her life.

Some spell, anything too certain not to be trusted, but once it happens, it's already too late and has always been too late, erasing all that came before.

Medea. She says her name aloud. Medea. Tries to remember. She reaches for a piece of her brother, a foot severed at the ankle, and presses it now to her breast, closes her eyes, tries to feel something for him, for her family, for her home, and feels nothing. Another life, someone else's life. Cold flesh, no different from the meat of an animal. This is strange power, too much power. Hekate no more than whisperings and rumor and blind earth compared with this, spells of a mole tunneling through nothing.

The day heating already. Her grandfather most powerful of the gods, giver of light and life and destroyer, also. But were there really none who lived before? How did the world become so populated? How can there be Minyae and Egyptians and Hittites and Colchians if the sun is her grandfather? How could Hatshepsut have ruled two hundred years back, and all the pharaohs before her, longest of lines? And how could every one of these Minyae be descended from the immortals? She understands almost everything they say because they share their language with the Mycenaeans, so she knows their story of themselves, each of them descended from a god, half god and half human. Yet they look like men. They sweat at the oars as the sun heats the air, they require food and water, they piss and shit. If they do descend from gods, they've inherited the weakest parts of that blood. As they pull, they stare at her breasts and legs and all think the same thing, same as any man in Colchis.

What Medea believes is this: that there are no gods. There is only power, and to hold power, you have to be descended from a god. In the end, this is the same thing. When you have that power, you do become a kind of god. Hatshepsut and every pharaoh before her.

Slaying her brother, destroying her father. These are acts of a god, acts that inspire fear and form myth. Gods do what cannot be done. And a woman can become a god easily because she is not allowed anything. She can become a thing of fear. Hatshepsut wearing a beard, both woman and man. And who would cross the priestess of Hekate? Who would stop a girl from wandering in the woods at night? Just the bare fact that she wants to be in those woods is terrifying to everyone.

But here among the Minyae she must start again. Chopping her own brother into pieces and licking his blood may be enough, or she may need to do more. Every one of them must fear her or she will become a slave.

Her brother's head, severed. Medea lifts it from beside her on the deck. She stares into his eyes, oddly intact, and chants to Hekate. She knows no Minyan will forget. Tales of how she invoked the soul of her dead brother or sent him to an underworld or might even be death herself. Let them tell it however they will.

What she remembers, though, is her real brother. His face still a face she loves. And she's broken by this, has to put his head down, sees him through all the years of their lives. She can play at power, but she is ruled by stronger things.

When they were children, they took one long journey with their father and their sister, Chalciope, in this direction, to Suppiluliumas the Hittite king in Hattusa, and saw carvings in stone of lions, sphinxes, warriors, and gods of the underworld. These carvings homes of the gods. This is what her brother deserves. She would carve a tomb for him with her bare hands, and this still would not be enough to atone.

She takes one last look at his face, her own face, and flings his head into the sea. Quick glance at the rowers to see them appalled, paused at their oars, horrified. Then she watches her brother's head fall away, bobbing in the waves a dark and strange creature. Hair contracting and flaring and contracting again like tentacles, propulsion in the new element. Looking down into these submerged heavens beyond where Helios can reach. Finding some account of his own short life written there in pattern and pressure and a different light made below. Heavy enough he should sink, but he doesn't. The surface of the water on fire from the sun, so she can't see her brother for long. Her father's ship not visible, lost somewhere far behind, and he should not be able to find this floating head, but she knows he will. She knows he will find every last piece.

They do not see her father's ship again all that long burning day and through the night and another day and another night. The wind dies in darkness, and they drop the sail, lowering the upper yard. Bumping and scraping as it falls, ponderous invention of brutes against the finer braid of stars above. These Minyae barbarians despite their belief in their own greatness.

Jason visiting afterward as half his men sleep and the other half pull at the oars. Visiting several times each night, and the smell of her brother increasing. The blood dried but flesh softening, rotting. They lie in this, most foul of wedding beds, and Jason himself smells as strongly musked as any beast in the field, but they must be with each other, a pull that comes

from their spines and curls them. She would pull him beneath
her ribs and keep him there.

He leaves for the oars again, and her grandfather climbs
into the sky again, and the sea is flat, without any wind at all.

Many of the crew still sleep, and those who pull at the oars
have slowed. They've become lazy. They think they're safe,
but Medea knows her father. They won't be safe until they
reach Iolcus and Jason's people and their fleet and army. He
won't stop until then.

Do not stop, she says in their language. Hurry.

They do not hurry. The Hieros mountains are in view now,
pale and washed out, without substance in this light. She
knows these mountains. Thermodon river just beyond. If
she still knows names, they are not far enough away to lose
her father.

The sun rises higher and the decks burn, planks so hot it
seems they could erupt in flame. No shade, no sail, no breeze.

The men wet and shining, skin burnt dark. Medea's skin
far whiter, turning red now, painful.

The water all around them on fire, too bright to look at, so
she closes her eyes and kneels on deck bowed down, hiding
from the sun, and waits for this to end. Each day on this boat
is longer than any day she has known before. Her grandfather's
path across the sky without measurable progress from hour to
hour, some punishment from him, to hold back the reins and let
her feel his wrath for how she has destroyed his line, the future
king cut into pieces. No forest to shield her, no fog or mist
or cloud or darkness or man-made shelter. A merciless god.

Jason brings her water every few hours, which is not
enough. Ship's rations, held below deck in a narrow space

above the ballast stones. She has seen them move aside the deck planks and reach below, and she wants to lie there in the shade. She believes she'll die soon if she remains in the sun. So she crawls forward and pulls up the short planks. The men watch her. Jason is rowing and says nothing.

She crawls into shadow below, and there is nothing soft. Stones and clay jars and tools: the sharp wide green blades of adzes, chisels, axes, whetstones, tongs, awls, drill bits, every hard and sharp and dangerous thing, raw ingots of copper and tin to make bronze. Smell of bilgewater and rot, mold. But in a narrow space between the rudder posts, she finds coils of rope, and here she can lie down. Rough fiber but not sharp or hard. A place to rest away from the sun.

Gentle rocking of a ship, even in a sea without waves, from the motion of the oars. Feel of that pull, sound of the waterline, a stream unceasing, and the ship could be going ten times as fast. It feels and sounds that way, escaping quickly, one of many illusions. They are moving too slowly. Her father is out there somewhere not sparing his men.

The hull feels as if it is burrowing, as if they are going deeper into the sea. A bird with its head straining downward, trying to dive, but only sliding along the surface.

She wakes, a hand at her ankle. She yanks her leg in panic, then sees it is Jason leaning in at the hatch. Your father, he yells.

She crawls over tools and stones, avoiding blades. The hull bucking beneath her, no longer calm. Her breath coming faster, expecting to see her father at the stern, about to leap aboard, but when she emerges, she sees no ship. The sun late in the day, falling, and a wind now against them, waves formed. Land close along their left side, the Hieros mountains rising above. They've come too close to land. A headland is directly ahead, and they'll need to go around it.

Where? she asks.

Jason points. Her father's ship is much farther from land, veered away from their path but correcting course now, angling closer, a dark shape on the water and a flash with every dip of the oars. Rowing quickly.

The Argonauts all at the oars now, no sleeping.

Fools, she says in their language. You stupid fools.

They're trapped. She hasn't been to sea before, but even she knows they're trapped against this headland. It should be obvious to anyone. And dropping a piece of her brother into the water will do nothing now. Her father's ship no longer following behind. Fools, she says again. You will all die.

She walks forward between their ranks, and if she had a whip, she would beat them. They cower from her, look down at the deck, pull at their oars. Boys, not men. Descended from sheep, not from gods. Your fathers fucked ewes and lambs, she yells at them. Smeared out on the earth and even your four-legged mothers walked away and left you.

At the bow, she raises her arms to the bare blue sky that has birthed wind without cloud and calls on Hekate. Hear me now, she says. Hear me now more than any time before, more than any time to come. Too much to promise to a god, Medea knows. Fuel this wind and make every oar slip. Build these waves and drive my father all the way back to his shores.

Medea shapes the wind and waves with her arms, pulls water up from the deep, works in the invisible element. Wind unseen. Its raw power, closest we come to feeling the gods.

Wrath and a willingness to destroy all, and the source of it endless, coming from the edges of the world.

Medea clings to the bow post as the fury increases. Waves breaking white, tops flattened in gusts, the water streaked. A haze that is water blown in the air, lowest form of cloud, purest form, salt cloud.

The Argonauts pull as fast as they can, the headland abreast, pounding of waves against rock. They're no longer making any progress against wind and wave. Only slipping sideways, closer and closer. Jason stands between the rudders at the stern, grim, understanding too late.

Knife-edged stone in strips and furrows dark on top and blackened in the surge, waves sucked away and sweeping forward again, spray flung higher than their ship, the headland shaped like an eel, long and thin, swimming closer, needle toothed and greedy.

If they don't make it around this point, they'll be trapped against shore, in a small bay, unable to escape.

Her father's ship angling closer to land but still much farther out. Oars ripped into the air as his bow rises, submerged again as it crashes down in a great plume of spray. Rolling, also, heavily to the side, and as his bow comes up again, it rolls out toward sea and is blown down until his ship is sideways and spinning. Medea laughs. Hekate doing exactly what she's asked, blowing her father back. Dark one, she yells into the wind. Beautiful one. First among gods.

Medea takes her knife and makes a slit across her forearm, raises her arm into the wind and lets her blood fly back over the Argo and its crew. For you, she calls to Hekate. All of my blood for you, always.

The surge beside the Argonauts now, a great trough in close, spray reaching their decks, and they are complete fools. They would row until the wood breaks up beneath them, until they are flung into the water and torn and impaled on these teeth like great urchins and starfish come from another world. But then Jason commands they stop rowing, and they all watch dumbly and hang on as the ship falls backward and the bow dives down in the trough and is blown inland, sideways, missing rocks by less than an arm's length. Water at the bulwark, nearly coming over, the ship leaning, but it comes upright again, and they've cleared. Hekate helping fools, beneath her.

I'm sorry, Medea tells her, and she opens a cut on her other arm and bleeds over both sides of the bow then walks back between the oarsmen with her arms raised, bleeding over each of them and finally over the helmsmen, who try to duck away. Fools, she says. You don't know who has saved you.

Her father spinning, too far from land to anchor, being blown all the way back to where he began.

Let this blow all night, if you favor us, Hekate. Let the wind only grow.

The Argonauts pull hard for this harbor, already in less wind and much smaller waves, making way again. Impossible to believe the fury of only a few moments before. The waves following, curving around the point, but softened. Wind confused, indirect, blown back from every direction in isolated puffs.

Calmer water ahead, protected pool, the slope rising steeply above, and Helios hidden behind, falling. The light on the Hieros mountains golden. All lost and then nothing lost. The ship capable again, gliding easily, and Medea can see small goatherds' huts along the shore, sticks piled against stone, a large fig tree planted close, and pathways leading into forest. A chance to leave the ship, a respite and shelter, though her father may have sent riders down the coast. They're too close to be safe from him.

The Argo built supposedly with the help of the goddess Athena, who watches over Jason, but it sags to the left, lopsided, and this is perhaps what saved it, turning the bow toward shore instead of to sea. Hobbled and fortunate. Ship of brute thieves trying their luck.

Four of them at the bow now, struggling with a great anchor stone, heaving it over the side and hopping out of the way as the line runs. Ripping over the bulwark. And what if the stone does not find bottom? They have no idea how far it must fall. Everything they do a blind faith flung into the void. Coming to Colchis knowing nothing, and if not for Medea, they'd already be strung in the trees.

Jason has promised to make her his queen when they return to Iolcus, and if he does not, she will destroy every last one of them.

The stone hits bottom, their luck holding, and the line is made fast. The ship rocks gently in the leftover curve of waves and spins slowly in the breeze.

Jason raises his arms to Athena, thanks the goddess for safe passage, and his men do the same, and no one thanks Hekate. No one thanks Medea.

The Minyae carry amphoras of wine from the hold and eye the edge of that forest, soft pine straw and goatherds' huts and a night away from the oars. Fifty of them, a horde working together like ants, carrying food and water and wine and their weapons, shields of ox hide and ashen spears, all ferried in this one tiny skiff that can hold no more than six men.

The light pink on the mountains, its previous gold impure and fading. The sea churned in white and darkened by spray, gray band in which her father is lost, oars reaching and finding no hold. A world removed, no more than rumor. Once you leave, you can no longer believe the sea.

They row her to shore with Jason. His men are gathering wood for a great fire, dismantling the huts of the goatherds, using their homes for fuel. Thieves always.

Strange light, all things illumined from their own sources, a light that lives in the air itself and seems not to come from the sun. Jason as he walks ahead of her seems not to touch ground, born of air only. No weight or substance. The entire world is tilting, the earth levering up, the rolling of the ship remaining inside even as they walk on land. Strange effect, and how long will it last? Will the world ever come upright?

Medea reaches to the side for balance, but there's nothing there. A man laughs at her, points, and other men laugh. Jason takes her arm, pulls her along over short grasses and flowers white and yellow then pine needles and exposed roots, and lays a sheep's hide on the ground. She sits, still spinning, lies back on the sea-blown earth, closes her eyes and caves away into endless falls.

When she wakes, there is a great fire on the shore against the night, and men singing. Dark forest come close, gathering, trunks appearing and fading, pulsing in firelight. The farthest trees the most nimble, impossible to track.

Medea rises, no longer dizzy, and walks uphill into this forest that extends from her own. Same sound of wind high and sourceless. Same weight of shadow. Her own dark form extending before her, longer than the ship, held to the earth, unable to free itself. This the highest mystery of all, what binds. What keeps the trees rooted, keeps shadow from rising. Hekate, unlock this, Medea says. Show me how to unlock all that binds. Let me separate shadow from ground.

Her forearms burn from sacrifice, pulsing, but no longer bleed. She holds them high as she walks, shows Hekate her offering. Home of the dark one, this forest that extends to every land and beyond to lands unknown. But in order to hear Hekate, it must be quiet, and all Medea can hear is the stupid boasting of the drunken Argonauts, shouting and quarreling, so she turns downhill and descends upon them.

Staggering around the fire holding their bowls of wine, slapping and grabbing at each other, most of them naked, singing half a dozen songs at once.

Golden bodies, thickly muscled from the oars, carved hollows, each broad back cleft by a deep valley, high sided and ridges beyond, piled and piled. Round swell of shoulders and wide chests. Legs rippling, flat-sided muscle. Some lie with each other reversed and swallowing, others mount, and all are swaying. Some are wet from the sea, most have bathed in oil, slick and glistening. A vision Medea would never have imagined, would never have been allowed to see. The most beautiful forms in firelight.

They should not be used for war, she thinks. They should be used only for this. But they've forgotten who saved them. There is no altar for Hekate, no offerings, no sacrifice, and though Hekate may be only rumor and story and shadow and nothing that can become angry, Medea's power is in Hekate and so all will worship her.

Hekate! she screams. Hekate!

They shrink away, all of them, stumbling from this sudden fury. She holds her arms high and chants to the goddess, takes a piece of wood and beats at the fire, pounds flame until at one end of this great pit there are only coals. Then she steps onto the coals, dances barefoot, and the heat brings her closer. She charges at the flames where they still rise, falls back, charges again, invokes all that would fill the air, leaps free and grabs Jason and pushes him to the ground, makes him kneel to this fire and to Hekate. The Argonauts follow, and those too drunk to understand she pushes to their knees, makes them bow and thank Hekate for their deliverance. She takes a firebrand from the coals and beats them with it, breaks it over one of their backs then chooses another. They will not dishonor her god.

Medea clubs them with flame and hot coals that shatter and are flung into the night like stars burning in a smaller sky. She takes an amphora, smashes it down onto rock, and the dark wine spatters them and hisses in the fire. Let them be painted the color of blood.

They whimper and cower and wait for Hekate to rain fire, while Medea beats and burns and brands them all, marked forever. Then she runs into the forest and when she's far enough away she falls panting to the forest floor and laughs. Iolcus will be hers. She will destroy Pelias, king of the sheep-men. Then she will rule beside Jason, and he will decide nothing. The Mycenaeans, too, will learn to obey, and the Athenians, and all others in that land. All will kneel to their barbarian queen.

Hekate, Medea says. She lies back in pine straw and looks up through the trees into stars. The men and their fire a glow below, a wavering. Show yourself. Live in my body. Take my form. If you have breath, let it be mine.

The treetops lunging like flame in this wind, a roar not unlike fire. Invisible flame, devouring nothing, sign only of what burns in another world.

33

The wind shrieks all through that night, Hekate veering close and vanishing and descending on them again. Whistling through rocks along the ridge and bending the forest low. Fury in its purest form, undeniable. The sea a white froth against black, growing. The Argo spinning in the harbor, leaning in gusts, rocking from surge.

Medea watches from the ridge, wanting the full fury, looking down on the fire below and bodies and the Argo lit broadside and ripple of waves lit golden.

Stars above, no cloud. Not a storm that can be understood, not cold, only Hekate's hot breath and will, and Medea consumed. She screams into the night so the men will know her as fury itself, flying all around them, in the forest, on the ridge, close by along the shore. She screams from each place then moves again. They must fear her enough to bring that fear to Iolcus. Every Iolcan will have spent this night here, cowering by the fire, after Medea raised the seas and wind and drove her father back. Even Pelias will fear.

Medea faces the blast, looks to the dark side of the headland where waves crash against exposed shore. Spray that reaches even to where she stands, water shattered and made into air, and this is what she would do, break all that is and reshape it.

Medea, she calls into the wind. I call on you, Medea. Fury. First among gods. I do this for you.

She walks along the ridge with her arms held high, and she is the wind. She has flung her father back to his shores and whipped the sea, and her feet will crush this spine of rock below if she desires.

Dark one, she says. Medea destroyer of kings. Medea ruler of all.

34

Scrub and bare rock, too much wind here for trees. Salt spray. End of the headland, blown, exposed, and she would whip this sea, master even the elements. This is what a king must believe. Her father the same. What's happening now can make no sense to him. After this, he will want to punish the air itself.

Gods hidden in water and land and air. The sea god somewhere in these waves, a great darkness forming beneath and churning, or breaking the surface somewhere at the edge of these waters and blowing. Impossible to say how all is formed. Giants beneath her now, encased in rock, waiting to break free. She would see them revealed. See them rise and walk, earthborn, earliest of gods. Unthinking, the moving of mountains, walkers rooting again and the headland now in a new place, mountains reshaped, needing new names.

All that is human far too small, and it is nothing to rule it.

Medea screams again for the Argonauts and runs back along the ridge, tearing at brush, stumbling in loose rock but staying upright, descending into trees and slipping in loose needles, flinging herself to the other side of this forest above them, screams and collapses, panting. They will be watching for her in the air now, in flight over the water.

She has done this to her brother for as long as she remembers, terrifying him. And yet still he came to her whenever she called, even when she held a knife. He trusted her. Disbelief when his throat was cut. No attempt to fight. She held his head in both hands as he died, talking to him, telling him she was sorry. Death not quick, and blood everywhere. So much blood in him, covering her, and his eyes still alive, looking into hers.

A future king, though she was firstborn, and she will need to learn to feel nothing when she kills kings.

Medea lies down under the trees and wants to sleep, but she can smell her brother, rotten flesh everywhere, on her arms, in her hair, all along her back. Bathed in his blood. Stink also of Jason and sweat and sex. So she walks down to the shore, away from the fire, and steps carefully in darkness over sharp rocks, eases into the warm black sea. She screams once more for the Argonauts, then she closes her eyes and submerges beneath the waves into stillness. This is where she would sleep. Arms and legs suspended, body weightless, no sound. She opens her eyes and sees stars, waves her arms and they curl around her, flung in currents invisible. Blackness and no light from above, only these constellations. She flings herself back, kicks and sees her body made a constellation, outline of her hips and legs. Tries to grab one of these stars, but they are somehow beyond reach. All around her and impossible to touch.

She rises for breath and descends again. A world withheld until now. Told not to swim at night in the sea and never taken on a boat at night. Bathing only in the day, in the river, cold water without stars. How is it she never wandered from the forest to the sea in all those hundreds of nights? What else lies close to us that we haven't yet seen?

She rubs along each part of her skin to remove blood and rot, and what washes off is only light, appearing and winking out again. Impossible to believe blood is real. She may wake to find she's done nothing, betrayed nothing, and there are no remains.

She wakes to the sound of axes. All through the forest around her, sharp over the howling of the wind. The sun shunted by sea-blown spray. Hekate unceasing, and the wind still hot, with no cloud, air warped and darkened. Her grandfather struggling to rise higher.

The Minyae building on the shore, wearing very little and slick from oil and sweat. She finds Jason beside fallen trees stripped of branches.

For Hekate? she asks.

For Hekate, he says.

And what will you sacrifice?

Jason looks around, spreads his arms to show there's nothing here. No goat or lamb.

Hekate needs blood, she says.

Jason looks out to sea.

Waves white and broken in water turned green. Medea wonders if the sea is ever the same. There's no sign of her father.

Your own blood then, she says, grabs his arm, shows the cuts on her own arms. She points at him and his sailors. All of you.

Jason nods, and she can tell he's afraid, which is good.

She pulls out her knife with its green bronze blade and handle of deer horn, carved with the face of Helios. I will make the cuts, she says.

Each will kneel before her and say the name of Hekate, and she will release their blood and chant above them, their priestess. There will be no more mention of weak Athena.

She leaves Jason, walks into the forest with a goatskin for gathering. The Argonauts afraid to look at her as she passes. Turning back to their chopping.

She climbs quickly to the ridge and disappears over the other side, and all is too dry. Another small ridge leading up toward the Hieros mountains, denser forest, gullies and canyons in shadow.

She could live here. Never return to Jason, never return to her father, live only in the forest, away from all others. But there would be no one to rule.

Steeper slope, and she has to walk. The trees reddish in this morning light, all standing waiting, bent and blown, obedient.

The ridge thinning, exposed rock, and she cuts lower across the slope, beneath cliffs. Farther inland, toward larger mountains, where there will be water, dense forest damp and rotting.

The forest will remake her, as it always has. Breath and blood and wind and isolation. The simple act of walking and hearing only her own footsteps. But there must be water, also, and the sound of water, a return to what she knows. Displaced now, hollow.

Medea runs again, realizing how far she must travel today. The larger mountains and thicker forest not close. And she must not be caught alone. Hittites farther inland, an empty place here, she's always been told, but those goatherds' huts belong to someone.

Fear the best way to run, endless fuel. She imagines men with spears running after her, and she no longer touches ground. She's done this all her life, chased by phantom men. Wearing masks like her father, faceless, soundless, apparitions relentless and always coming closer.

Her father a threat from the very beginning, an enemy before she was born. The power of every king balanced by a terrible prophecy. Her father told by his father, Helios, that his own children would scheme against him. Pelias warned about Jason. Even the gods do not like the power of kings. Even the gods would have them destroyed.

Kings always blind. Her father not considering his daughters, believing a threat only in a son. Daughters to him no more than a tool to bind other peoples through marriage. Unwilling emissaries, their will never considered. Soon enough she would have been sent to the Hittites or

Egyptians or anyone else and forgotten, never to return home.

Outcast. This is what she has chosen, and it would have been chosen for her anyway. Her father an enemy later if not now, marriage not powerful enough to prevent war.

It should have been her father she cut into pieces, hacking at his limbs, all power gone, but she loves him, too, only because he's her father. Cruel trick of the gods, to bind children.

Deeper into the forest, and Medea runs without looking back. She knows she will never be lost. She holds the shape of every pathway inside her, the shape of mountains. All felt and known for as long as she can remember. No moss here, no ferns, no cliff faces covered in bright green, no streams with gold, and the trees are not the same, but she would recognize any forest, even if all were changed. And she will find wetter ground here. She will find what she needs for Hekate: moss and root and mushroom and berry and bark and rot and spoor and what lives in these places blind and trackless and mute and forgotten.

On the next ridge she finds spruce, pushes her way through lower dead branches, coiled, snapping against her, and follows game trails down into a ravine.

Shadowed and the sound of wind lost somewhere above. Earth dark, rich, breaking beneath her feet. Steep slopes and she's sliding with every step.

Cold ravine, outside time, a cleft in the mountain, one of the silent places where Hekate waits, god without breath. A feeling of being watched. Air still and weighted to the ground and the sound of water sourceless, coming from every direction, even from above.

A place of fear but home to Medea, black earth, black trees, black water, black rock. She descends to where the water tunnels below high banks, roots exposed and close enough for one bank to reach the other. She could leap across.

She kneels here in damp earth and feels the mountainside tipping vertical. She lies at the edge and reaches down where she can't see, reaches under an overhang to lightless places hidden in root and web and feels for any moving thing, comes up with spiders on her hand, bulbous black and one of them pregnant, engorged. Medea brushes them into the goatskin bag, presses the sides gently to kill but not ruin. Legs moving still, reddish on their undersides, faces hooked and eyes limitless. She finds one pair, looks closer, and finds another and another, a being living in darkness yet covered in eyes. Strange fur all along the edges, fur for something made of darkness and without any need of warmth.

She reaches again through root and dirt and web and claws into the roof of this cavern, comes out with a fist of dark rot and a few small white worms, pale and nearly translucent. Seekers waving in the air, reaching blindly toward the heavens. Then a larger pale head emerging, like a human baby, hairless and slick, as big as her thumb. Reddish and veined, fragile just like a baby's head, ugly for being so bare and moist. Small black eyes. A yellow pincer mouth like an upper lip swollen in deformity. Yellow legs and a segmented body, black banded below. She has seen one of these battle before, killing a wolf spider that would have filled the palm of her hand.

Most ugly of all that crawls. She must kill it carefully, leave all intact, because she will hold this creature on her tongue as each of the Argonauts comes up to her. They will see her face and then this smaller face and the insect legs.

She pins it down with one hand and reaches for her knife, delicately pushes the point into the back of the head. White pus forming and frantic clawing of every leg, then all is still.

Monstrosity always near, and fear easy to wake. The Argonauts will be changed tonight.

Medea crawls to a rotten tree uprooted and fallen across the forest floor, dismembered, its meat reddish and tracked and inhabited. Termites, their frail wings. She pinches their heads, adds several to her bag. Her fingers unspeakably large, she tears apart a mountainside, exposes caverns and tubes filled with bodies. Finds what she was looking for, slack black skin of a scorpion in a cavern, tail hidden. Thick arms, brutish. Arms of an infant, fatty, segmented, held close.

How it reached this cavern a mystery. Deep inside the log, pathways too narrow, and what will it do here? Wait in darkness forever?

Tombs in a wall, arranged in lines as if written here, carved into stone, layer upon layer. Some record of a place unknown, preserved by an unseen hand. Order in the world, even in places buried. Prophecy the art of reading these signs. Scorpion among termites, wrath waiting as all is eaten. Prophecy always about decay.

She will wear this scorpion as a bracelet, its legs curling around, and use this hand to hold their forearms in place. Pale insect head on her tongue, black infant arms of the scorpion on her wrist, feel of the knife and vision of blood. They will believe this to be the most ancient of rituals, from a darker past before telling, and they will fear her as they fear their own ancestors.

But Medea knows no ritual is sacred. No ritual ancient. All are made in their own time. No one taught her Hekate's rites.

Her knife edged in bronze golden from use, dull green across its face. Thick and imperfect and hovering close to the dark low head so flat it can't really be seen, only a part of the rumpled shelf of body, cradled by thick pincers obscenely swollen.

The termites in panic, dragging their wings, climbing the face of their destroyed home, strange waddling walk.

Blade upside down, carving slowly into the decayed roof above, point nearing the head, and still no movement. Red dust falling on soft black platoo.

Medea stabs, and the scorpion arches, pincers thrown wide, tail curved high, hooked, and the floor fails and he tumbles close to her knees. She yanks back, stabs again and misses. The scorpion fast, gone backward, flat curve gliding away, but she stabs him through his midsection, pins him to the ground. He flexes and his tail stings the blade, last spasms, soundless. Pain unregistered, unrecorded.

Collapse of a form difficult to believe. Where did the scorpion come from? Unlike anything else in this forest, born of what dream.

The tail in her fingers still pulsing, wicked point hooked and reddish. She presses it down against the body, wonders if he can feel his own sting. Legs curling in, death slow. Until all is slack, and she slides him off the knife into her bag.

She follows the stream in its hollow, walking ground that could cave beneath her, and looks for mushrooms for the

Argonauts, to make them see. She will change shape and grow by the fire, become impossible to locate, a leering image of fear. She plucks bits of fern and moss, finds droppings she can't identify, spoor of something larger, gathers a few pellets. A sense of being watched, and her breath shallow. Listening, but all is covered by the water beside her. All that would encase coming closer still.

Leaves and needles and old branches rotting. Mushrooms in clusters near the bases of trees and on banks that have fallen away but not the right mushrooms, and she doesn't know whether she'll recognize what grows here.

She moves deadfall, an old branch, and a salamander kinks and runs toward the water but she's faster, grabs him and holds him close to peer at that sealed mouth, overwide, and slack throat. Eyes without any depth that can be known, bottomless and vacant, numb even at extinction. Belly and squat legs edged in red, otherwise black, as if all creatures must be this, all burrowing upward from some underworld to wait on the surface or just under. Skin moist and not meant for air, for sun. Half-born.

She presses her thumb at his throat until he yanks and dies, sets him carefully in the goatskin and continues on. It could be that no human has ever walked here before. No path, no sign, no trees cut. Wanderers, and so perhaps no forest is untouched, but this air feels unbreathed.

The stream rises in small falls and pools and the banks no longer overhang, no longer so deeply etched. Rotted wood and rock and moss and coming closer to the familiar. Medea finds a colony of mushrooms on a decayed black branch at the stream's edge. Perfect round caps on short stalks. Domed, bulbous, and so plain looking, a smooth light brown, but these are the right ones. Gatekeepers to the other world.

The Argonauts will begin a new voyage, she says.

The sound of her voice too loud and exposed. She looks around, waits and listens, but there is only the water, made of a hundred sounds and enough to erase all else.

She takes every mushroom, every stalk and bulb until only white circles remain among the bright green moss, a sign unreadable and seen by no one.

She is running out of time. Far away from the shore, and the sun past its peak. She won't lose her way in light, but she could easily lose her way in darkness.

The goatskin filling. She needs root still, and berries, but there will be no berries here.

She can't take the same path back. All her life she's avoided that, always making a circle, afraid to return for what she might find waiting along the way. The sense always of being followed.

So she climbs toward the sea. Steep and the sky rolling away, the mountain growing. Sound of wind, in the distance at first and then all around her, and she crests, every tree surging, and falls again into another canyon.

She rises and falls without thought, her mind going flat on every journey, return to the earliest form, before language. Only listening, aware of scent and movement. Same as any beast.

She returns in darkness along the shore. Two great fires, flames taller than the men. An altar between. High platform for the priestess, poles reaching above, and a lower platform where the men will kneel. The Argo spun and lit, waves undiminished, the sea covered in windblown white, Hekate untiring.

Smell of cooking. They've found some meat, and instead of sacrificing to Hekate they're keeping it for themselves.

Medea moves in close, hidden by trees, and screams, sees them twist and yank, searching for the source. She steps forward into firelight, raises her arms, chants.

Song of Hekate, song of fear. Song of all that waits. Edges of the world approaching, low moan building. The men fall away from their cooking and the fire. Each of them muscled and far larger than she. The one in bearskin holding an enormous ax. But they cower.

Medea rolls her eyes back, twists her mouth and moans and screams. She shakes, calls for Hekate, and falls to the ground.

No human sound, the men still. Sound only of the fire and shrieking wind.

Fear builds with time. Fear is made of waiting, so Medea doesn't move. Let them wonder whether she's dead. And when she rises, let them wonder who she is, Medea or Hekate.

Waves breaking then blown, flashing in darkness, decapitated and scattered. Medea curls her back, a jolt of movement as if she were being ripped inside. Then she rises, hunched, faced away toward the sea. Her fingers are held wide like claws and she turns slowly, keeps her chin pinned against her chest, face hidden by her hair, takes one step and another and knocks their spit of meat into the fire and screams.

Hissing of fat and the fire darkened, a deep red down low. Smell of flesh charring. They have several bronze cauldrons boiling, one with fish for soup, another with bark for tea. She takes a branch and tips the soup onto the ground at their feet. Flesh opaque white and torn, thrown on this shore as if the sea itself had boiled, scattered and left to rot. There will be no food.

She takes the salamander from her goatskin, holds it high by its tail, thick curved fin like a fish, a half creature monstrous, unbelonging, and bites off the head, spits it into their tea, then lets the body join.

She raises her knife for all to see, cuts her arm and bleeds into the cauldron. She presses along the arm to hurry the blood, sucks and spits into the brew, adds her mushrooms and moss and spoor. She cradles the spiders in her bloody palm and walks close to the men.

Slack cheeks, open mouths, fear and hatred too. Dark eyes. Jason as foreign as the rest, child-king.

Black globe of a pregnant spider revealed then thrown in. Medea stirs with a stick and the slick brown heads of the mushrooms well at the surface. She chants to Hekate in her own tongue. Destroyer, break the knees of these Minyae, make them worship and beg. Distort them tonight and make them see shapes of fear, let them know me as fear. Take the world they know away from them and leave them alone and whimpering.

She takes one of their bowls, dips it into the soup, makes sure there are several mushrooms. Then she fills the rest as they step forward. No man looks at her. They stand waiting until they are an army, each facing the fire, holding a bowl and waiting for a command. Every instinct in them the instinct of a slave. Jason is last, and he is no braver than the rest, looking down.

Medea steps to the altar, her back to the sea, flames before her and the men beyond. Hekate, she says and tips her head for them to drink, and every man does it. They drink and chew until each holds his bowl empty before him in both hands, facing her like fifty small shields. Medea smiles. They are too easy. Then she folds down over her knees, cocooned, silent, faceless, waiting. Let them be lost.

Fire and sea. Voices endless and opposed. Fire always coming closer, the sea forever receding. Wind awakening both. Hekate in fire, no steady pulse, no surge and fall but panic after panic and more voices beneath and more beneath those, all buried half in the ground and writhing above, muffled and consumed. Smaller gods just as greedy.

Shrieking overhead, and Medea smiles. There could not be a more perfect night for this. A night in which none may find shelter. All the world distorted.

She waits until she hears them retch, waits longer still for the visions to begin. They will be crawling now, and they will want to die, and everything will begin spinning from the inside. As they suck for air, every terror will be let in.

Moaning, sound of the terrified, and she rises to see them on the ground, clutching their bellies, writhing in dirt, an army collapsed. Poisoned and made new.

She steps down to the fire, takes a thick burning branch and throws it among them, watches them curl away. You will burn, she tells them in their language. You will all burn, for Hekate.

She holds the scorpion by its tail, dull black shape of fear, and walks among them with its body hanging, pincers and flat plates, headless and ancient, brings it close to each face, sees their mouths twist in horror. The scorpion still alive for them. All night they will be chased by shapes in the air, living shapes, the gates opened.

She lets those legs touch a shoulder, the back of a knee, a face, and the men scream. She climbs on top of Jason, presses down against him, sets the scorpion on his bare chest. He doesn't dare move. Trembling. Then she moves on, straddles another man, and another. Let them think of her now and remember her always with this scorpion. She takes each man in her hand so he'll feel his desire. All ritual is desire. There can be no god without desire.

Medea stands, the only one standing, and returns to her altar, calls to the men. Give your blood now to Hekate. She curses them in their own language. If you ever betray me, let your sons be slaughtered and no seed fall from you again. Let your land die and your people be forgotten and no sign remain and no gods.

They crawl forward. She drops to her knees on the higher platform. The slick smooth head of the infant on her tongue.

Jason is first, struggling onto the lower platform, falling sideways and righting himself. She can tell when he sees the insect on her tongue, sees him jerk. But she takes his wrist and slashes her knife across his forearm. Skin yellow in fire-light, then the blood wells red, deepest of hues in darkness. She rolls her eyes back and sways before him with knife and scorpion. Let him never forget.

In the morning, the wind has died down, Hekate appeased. The men return to the ship, each lost in memory of visions that are not possible and cannot be reconciled to the day-lit world. Darkness remaining.

Each man fearing the air itself, and his own flesh and what might be harbored there. No talking among them. None dare look at Medea.

Sagging Argo, built by weak men and a weak goddess. Heavy and blunt bowed compared to her father's ship. Darkened wood eaten by sea worms and slathered in pine pitch, gaps in every seam, wood forced together without skill. Laden now with fresh water but no meat. They will have to fish.

The men tired and looking toward waves no longer white but still strong, blown from the far end of the sea. They don't raise the anchor yet. All are aboard, all is ready, but they sit and wait and bake in the sun.

Hours of this, Medea on the stern where her brother's remains have fused to the wood, dried and shrunken and infested with white maggots. Most of him still here, almost enough to fashion a man. Missing a thigh, a forearm, a head, but the rest intact.

The deck too hot to touch. They must stay exactly where they are and not move, each on an island of wood cooled by sweat. The breeze uncertain, in puffs from one direction then another, in back eddies, and they feel its heat when it comes from land.

Helios high overhead when they finally pull up the anchor stone, four of them, wet rope darkening the deck. Others have already begun rowing, turning the bow toward sea.

The boat a heavy weight dragging, water swirling from the oars without effect. Slow lumbering creature filled with rock. The distance to Iolcus unknown and unbearable.

Jason a stranger, standing just before her on deck but distant, commanding the helmsmen to stay close to shore, crawling along the headland toward the point. The sea divided, darker line for wind and wave, the storm died down but not yet gone.

The altar on shore, remaining for all to see. Great blackened fire pits. But soon enough, the goatherds will tear everything apart, rebuild their huts. So the next altar will be of stone. When they arrive in Iolcus, Jason will build an altar to Hekate in marble, and a temple larger than any other. No other god will come before Hekate, no other priestess before Medea.

The headland extending, but finally they reach the edge and feel the wind. The men soaked in sweat and cooling now, a welcome breeze. Waves buried and sucked into dark rock and shredded into white. The boat pitches and rolls.

The men row hard, waves driving them back, the point remaining beside for too long, but they do finally clear and Medea watches the headland recede, searches the sea for any sign of her father's ship. His golden mask and spear and shield. She imagines he could appear over the water without any ship at all, standing just above the waves, coming closer, unstoppable. Eyes visible behind that mask, gray and cold.

Creaking of the hull beneath her, bent and shuddering, and for all its weight it feels fragile, bowed and ready to snap. They will find only waves below their feet, and they will not be like her father. They will sink down, no sign left, and her father will search forever until he becomes a god. Gods made of any action unresolved. Her grandfather in his chariot. Hekate in wind and fire. The sea god in waves. Nute swallowing without end and always giving birth again. Her father searching for the pieces of his son. The fear they have for Medea must also be without end.

The rudders loose, bound by thick rope now stretched. Resting on forked posts, lashed together but flexing with every wave. The men on the tiller handles braced and struggling. The lower lashing at deck level slick, worn black, pulled outward then upward and yanked in tight, shaft knocking against the hull. Blades in the water below trembling and diving into wave after wave, submerged then almost clear, great dark wooden faces, only a thin lower edge trailing.

The sea erupting beneath them in great boils and upwellings rimmed by foam and hissing. Every pattern and shape shrinking from every edge into unknown centers. Glimpse of the deep in each clear welling, fibrous with light, muscled. What might live down there none can say. Something large as mountains.

The Argonauts fight the sea, and it's clear they left too early. Only as the sun goes down do the waves diminish at all, the headland still visible in the distance, their progress far slower than if they had walked along the shore.

One of the men comes to the stern near Medea to fish in last light. A rough net weighted with stones. He ties a line to a rudder post, his fingers swollen and scraped, innumerable small scars and cuts. A young man with old man's hands. He ties a second line to an oar loop and flings the net overboard, beautiful pattern in flight, a practiced throw, the stones swirling out into a perfect circle just as they hit water.

Dragged behind them, and easy to see how slowly they're going. Net bowed and sinking, rising again as the stern is pushed up by a wave. The surface become silver, opaque, molten, as if the sea could be reforged every day, great ingot of tin melted down each night, this fisherman casting his net to capture impurities. Pulling at some guide line now, and when the net rises again, it's taken the form of a shallow basket, wide rounded mouth, black spider work amid silver, then submerged.

Only metal can look cold as it burns, and no other liquid can be so heavy. This sea could break the world, some platform below snapping and folding and all rushing down, seas draining and the shore slipping. Who can say what's below or what this world rests on.

The fisherman the only Argonaut to work in the invisible, the only one to pull at a line and feel the unseen. Long-bearded but young, worn and new, burnt darker than the rest, hidden. He should have led this voyage. Medea would have found him more interesting than Jason. She's realized by now she left Colchis for more than love. She would make her own kingdom. What she felt as love, a kind of madness, was also the thrill of her freedom.

Rough fingers with their own life, feeling what pulls at the line, testing the weight and making shape out of darkness, corollary forms. A mind dedicated to darkness, like her own.

When the net rises again, the basket has narrowed and come alive, molten spray as fish hit the back end, flap of tails and fins trying to leap free. If day were to come now, early, each form would be cast and frozen forever, curl of a spine and fin ribboned and water hanging above solid, immutable.

The fisherman tilts his head to the side as if listening. A still point. Gauging weight and balance. He hauls in quickly, muscles corded and bare and purplish, the light changing rapidly, no longer silver but bruised and dark, the sea made of flesh. Hauling in with quick strokes, perched on the edge and perfectly balanced, always upright, bearded and mute and rapt and trolling the great pools below. Thief and priest.

Ancient art. From time before telling, one of the first arts, older than her own. She puts her hand on his shoulder as he pulls, feels the ripple beneath the surface, and he does not pause. He is beyond reach.

The net rising now, stones clattering at the bulwark, and he grabs as if it were a throat, brings it closer and stands to haul upward, steps back quickly until all is on deck beside Medea, flash of scales blood silver and panicked, twisting, a dozen braids of light each pulsing on its own, mouths gasping and sliding away, loose pouch collapsing.

The fisherman kneels beside her again, his knife a dark shadow moving quickly. Each fish chopped and torn, entrails flung into the sea, scales scraped and gathering in great constellations among her brother's remains. Dusted with stars that come from blood and salt and all that is hidden and unknown. This is better than anything she could have imagined, perfect burial for a prince.

Joined, she says. You are a weaver.

But he slits and flings and chops and scrapes and pays no attention to her, lost in movement and the echo of that movement.

Endless night and endless day and night again, and no sign of her father, no other ship on this black water. World without light. No other humans, no gods. Only the unstill boat, sleep an impossibility, and the fickle wind, sliding along every edge of the world.

Blowing from the side now, enough breeze to sail, yards twisted, hanging over bow and stern, everything tipped, bulwarks dipping dangerously close to the waves. The crew gathered on the uphill side for weight, oars shipped. A time to rest, but fear of drowning prevents that. And fear of land, how close, and whether they might be blown onto it. Invisible in this night. A greater darkness somewhere down low, but with each blink the horizon changes and tilts and shadows reverse and no reference.

If the wind shifts, they will still keep it to their side and may sail straight into land, won't know they've turned. The truth is they have no idea what direction they're going. Each waits for land to rise up, for the hull gouged, and can hope only for a shore and not a small rock in the middle of the sea.

Fear living in close. In the hull and mast that might break, in the rudders, in the air that somewhere holds land, but mostly in the water. Rock and every creature unknown. No limit to the size of what can grow below. All animals on land known but always something new coming up from the depths.

Medea a priestess of darkness, and even she feels fear. Not the same as a forest. Great void waiting, and all that the mind can shape writhes and slips away and will return. Held suspended above that, exposed, dangling at the roof of the lower world.

The serpent in water form, side fins wide fans like wings, water dragon, jaws outsized for the body, distorted, long teeth and tiny eyes, devouring whatever comes near, and who can say how large it might grow? A mouth larger than this ship, and able to sense them, rushing toward them now.

Sharks, also, just below the surface, always waiting. No sea meant to be crossed, and all travel on it borrowed. Filled with abominations. Row after row of teeth on a shark. No eyes on a jellyfish, no face, mostly transparent, made of what? Eyes on an octopus, but how to make sense of the rest? Impossible forms, all beneath her now in a world without sun and perhaps without end. There may be no floor to this sea. If she dies here, she may sink and keep sinking. Medea can see herself submerged, outlined in those stars below, arms wide, turning slowly as she descends, hair pulsing above, and she falls and falls and is torn apart and devoured. No burial, no rites, only monstrous forms wrapped around her until there's nothing left.

The men say nothing. The previous night, there was a small fire in a cauldron on deck, fish roasted on skewers, but there's no food now, the deck tilted too steeply.

They wait in hunger and darkness and fear until finally one of them lights a torch. It will blind them. They won't be able to see any darker shape loom out of the general darkness. But the torch is lit anyway, and they continue to peer into nothing, and keep this light as a comfort, as a shield against fear, as all have done since there was first fire.

The sail brown linen in constant movement, lashed along the yards and straining, collapsing at one end then filled and straining again, slow breath, a kind of lung nearly as long as the ship. The yards swaying, men hauling on the lower lines at bow and stern. Thick mast with its bronze head and dozen eyes pierced by lines, a god torturing itself, tying its arms to its eyes and twisting in the night, single lunged and exposed, no ribs or skin to protect or conceal, bound and suffering, half-buried in the deck and struggling to stand as every line pulls downward.

Caught before this god, sailing over the abyss, Medea and the Argonauts awaiting their fates. God made of wood and air and linen, more alive and struggling than flesh. What animates rock and wood and water and air? Where does it come from, and can we find this place? Some fire from which every spark originates, a fire guarded, and what would happen if it were to escape? Every stone rising up, a thousand shapes coalescing in the water, the air itself thickening with forms, felt as we feel breeze but individual and able to enter us and leave again. Would we sense their shape even if we couldn't see? And what if light and darkness became animate? Pieces of light wandering in darkness, and black night found in the day.

Medea would take the Argonauts to this fire, make them row in whatever element to find the source. She would step into the fire, inhale and carry it within her. Then she would return to the inanimate world and choose what would have life.

With day they discover they've sailed away from shore, in exactly the opposite direction of what they feared. Helios rising to their right.

They turn downwind, swivel yards, and the deck flattens, wind no longer frightening. The sail billowing out front. All is calm and easy and their night just passed seems unreal.

Land far away now to the left, thin dark line as the sky lightens and the water goes white, land born between sea and sky and at this distance capable of submerging in either. The sailors don't like to be so far from shore. Helmsmen angling to close the gap. A place Medea had never imagined, breath of fear because the waves are so close and immediate and every small piece of water is like this, expanding all the way to the horizon, uncrossable. Panic of open space, something she's never felt before, and the ship is tiny. She could fall off at any moment.

Opaque sea, unbroken surface, a solid below with only its face shifting. This is her mind demanding safety, refusing depth and void. Weak, she says. Do not be weak like these sheep-men. But the fear remains.

Sun rising and hiding all beneath it. Her father could be gaining and they wouldn't see. Blind and running, they've lost time by sailing off course. The Argonauts have probably never sailed at night before. She's never heard of any ship sailing in darkness.

The wind a gift, blowing from behind, but a gift to her father also, and the Argonauts who are awake search the void toward Colchis as they wait. Most of them sleep. No rowing. The waves not large but the breeze steady, perfect conditions and a time to rest. Sound of the rudders, constant streams. Medea lies on deck near her brother, closes her eyes and follows sound into sleep.

Jason has stayed away. He does not return until that night, when they sail without torches. Perfect darkness. She cannot see his face even as she kisses him. He is known by weight and heat without shape. How demigods are formed. Women tricked. Gods coming down and hiding in darkness, pretending familiar shape, wanting their own image on earth.

How her grandmother lay with Helios was never told. Some dream continuing into day, holding light in her arms, eyes closed lest they burn. Her bedroom become the sun. All in Colchis must have seen this light, the heavens brought

close. One morning together, then held at a distance forever after, waiting for him to rise behind mountains and
extinguish into the sea and never come closer but ride the
farthest arc, untouchable. A bride able to gaze directly at
her groom only for the last moments each day, waiting
again each night.

The stories of her conflicting and erasing. Daughter of
Oceanus, an ocean nymph named Perseis, or she was someone else entirely, named Ipsia, or Eidyia, or Asterodeia, or
Neaera, or Eurylyte. Giving birth to a king who would erase
her, never tell her story, and claim only his father. Reduced
to a rumor. She may even have been killed. Aeetes born only
of the sun, great king without weakness, fearing only his son,
Apoyrtus, Medea's brother.

Medea wants to know her grandmother's art. Priestess,
weaver, singer. What was she? Did she dance in fire also?

No history before Medea's grandmother other than Titans.
No king this woman's father but instead the Titan Oceanus,
no prince her brother, no rule before her son. Aeetes would
be the first king. A strange land, Colchis, without history. A
people born suddenly out of the furrows or the sea and hung
in trees after death, a people without origin or destination,
existing only for a single king.

Jason would erase Medea. Use her to claim a victory, to
claim dominion over barbarian lands, use her to bear children, his heirs, of royal lineage on both sides, then cast her
away to be forgotten. She knows he would do this, and this
is what she must make impossible.

She clings to him now, held suspended over the deck, lost
in pleasure, but she won't forget.

What it would feel like to be ravished by a god, to hold a deity. All weight gone, held now as Jason holds her, but limitless strength. To surrender absolutely and know afterward that in your womb you carry something half divine that will live a greater fate, a shaper of entire peoples.

They lie panting afterward, her arms and legs still wrapped around him. Medea listens to the rudders, the sail, lines and hull creaking and rolling, listens for Jason's breath and heartbeat, a heartbeat she may need to end, years from now but no less relentless in its coming.

The deck hard. She's being crushed. So she pushes him off and he rolls to the side. Maggots and rot, invisible, occasional flash of fish scales catching some light otherwise unseen. Blind voyage again in darkness.

Jason leaves her and she sleeps again, too tired to be afraid of what waits below or follows close behind. When she wakes it is already day and they've come closer to land. On the same course still, wind behind, still no other ship. They might as well be the only humans, the rest of the world vacant.

The land growing slowly, rounded hills and forest milky in this overcast light, a dark white sky hung low. Medea's grandmother, if her name was Eidyia, may also have been Medea's mother. Oceanus the father of Medea's mother and also the father of Medea's grandmother, and the wife of Oceanus his own sister. Erasure. Medea comes from water and sun, and apparently that's all she is to know. The men are the sun and the women are water. Her mother and grandmother the same woman, appearing only to give birth then vanishing again, both Oceanids and born of another sea goddess, the Titaness Tethys, who is the same with simply another name. All of them the same, all melting into nothing and never known. Not one memory of any older generation of woman, and so it seems Medea and her sister could have sprung from water itself, or that only men exist.

The world emptied on this gray watery day, and it does feel as if Medea could be the only woman, or the same woman. She will have to make herself individual.

The shore is without sign. Too far to be known.

Medea eats fish roasted the previous day. The fisherman the one who is keeping them alive. He sits on deck and looks out at the waves, always watching the water. The surface somehow indicating what might lie below, but only to him. Opaque to Medea.

The men have learned how to wait through day after day at sea. They go into a kind of waking sleep, unmoving, not talking, their eyes open but not seeing her. Even Jason has no recognition. She could be made of air.

Not a single word spoken the rest of that long day, Helios hidden behind cloud and slowed in his passing, a day that could be a hundred days, then night which seems only an extension of the same day. Medea can no longer bear it, so she crawls below over rocks and tools blind until she reaches the coil of rope, feels the flex and creaking of the rudder posts on either side, a comfort, return to a kind of womb, a darkness held by a greater darkness, substitute for a mother never known, and is able to sleep.

Not far from shore now, searching for the entrance to another sea, slim passage difficult to believe, something from myth. How such a great sea could have only one small stream leading to another sea and then to an even greater sea beyond, as if the world could open itself larger again and again, unfolding without end. Jason and his Argonauts claiming to be the first ever to have passed through safely. The Symplegades rocks grinding every other ship to dust for centuries, but the Argo's passing fixed them in place forever, safe now. The stories these men tell about themselves absurd.

The forest thinned, drier, smaller trunks. Then the white curve of a beach, rare along this shore. A small hut at the edge of the sand, and then another, but no people, hiding perhaps.

The men alert, all awake now, ready to drop the sail, ready to take up oars, their spears and shields lying on deck beside them. Thracians at Lygos, on the far side of the passage, not to be trusted. They somehow must have allowed passage before, but apparently that doesn't mean they'll allow passage again.

Jason standing near her, between the helmsmen. The great bear-man at the bow holding his war hammer and shield, a warning to Thracians and anyone else.

Sail pulled to the side as they turn, the ship rolling in small waves. Enough breeze still. Every man hoping it will remain, wanting a fast passage.

Headlands and another small point, low and forested. The passage must be just beyond. She can see now the point on the other side and the settlement of Lygos, low walls and rounded dwellings on a hill, the land stripped and brown. Mud dwellers. Larger but less grand than Colchis. Her father's city the greatest on this sea.

The passage not as narrow as she had heard. Lygos farther away than she had imagined, shrunken in the distance, boats in a harbor just barely visible, tucked in along the shore. They've been seen by now, no doubt, but men at this distance too small, an impression only of the hillside itself shifting, some movement in the dirt.

Thracians have come to Colchis before, fishermen, dirty beggars wearing hides. Even their sails made of hides, not of linen. Using stones for knives. And more numerous than any other people on this sea.

Headlands blocking the wind now, sail gone slack. The Argonauts strike water with their oars, rowing hard, bending in unison. Helmsmen staying close to this shore, entering what looks like a long narrow bay.

Thieves always running, this is who the Argonauts are. Slipping along this far shore. The water calmer now, protected, and changed in color, turquoise, bright even under clouds.

The land curving, taking them closer to the harbor of Lygos, passage narrowing. The Argo moving faster now, helped along somehow by the gods. Going twice as fast as it has before, and Medea thinks the water itself must be moving, carrying them, because only the shore is passing quickly, not the water around them. Strange world. This water sucked toward the other sea, the sea god breathing in.

Fear. That at the end of this passage, the world collapses, all water drawn downward and the land, too, folding inward. Great waterfalls into a dark abyss, entire hillsides and forests falling through air, the Argo and its crew and Medea twisting endlessly, waiting for an impact that never comes. Medea knows this is not true, because the Argonauts sailed from Iolcus, the other side, and so there can't be any collapse. But she fears anyway, because of what she sees, all this water rushing somewhere, impossible if there isn't a fall at the other end. What she sees can't make any sense otherwise. Water in a level place doesn't rush.

And then she realizes something terrifying, that perhaps they've simply lied. Perhaps they've never been through this passage before. At the far end of her father's sea, beyond

Lygos, is a great river that leads eventually to another sea. A long passage, difficult, but they could have come from there.

Medea can hardly breathe. Panicking, and she considers jumping overboard, swimming for shore. Close enough still she might make it. Strange turquoise color, hiding all, and she doesn't know what might be waiting. Heavy-looking water. It could be too thick to swim in. She could be pulled under.

The men at the rudders having trouble steering, the Argo sagging sideways one direction then another, wallowing. Current moving too quickly, sweeping them along. Jason shouts at the oarsmen, has them quicken their pace.

Other rowers coming over the water, Thracian boats. Masts without sails, rowing into the wind, angling ahead to where the shores come closest to meeting. Lower boats, slim and light and fast and filled with men, tiny still in the distance but growing.

Jason takes one of the lines of the sail himself, thick line tied to the lower yard, and tries to find some wind, pulling in carefully, letting out, tugging again, trying to catch a pocket of air, something to help them along.

Medea eyes the shore again, near enough she might make it. If men swarm the deck and kill the Argonauts, she knows what waits for her, passed along from man to man, a slave the rest of her life if she lives through the first days. Water that would hold down and devour, men who would do worse. Small cliffs here, but she could climb, disappear into the forest, live alone hidden in ravines, work slowly back to her mountains.

There are no gods, only men. Hekate would not save her. There is no Hekate. Medea can feel the thinness of the air, the emptiness of the world, no one to call on. Empty invocations. And none descended from gods but only claiming origin in oblivion. All who came before have been erased, and Medea would guess not a few generations but a hundred generations or a thousand generations, ancestors mute and forgotten, born into the same brutal world of men rushing to the kill. Women always having to trick their way out of slavery, but she doesn't see what she can do now.

All the hours of their lives come down to these few minutes. Jason holds the thick line in both hands, gazes into the sail as if it were alive, beast that could be reawakened. Some shape, a bit of pull, then flattened again by their own headwind, moving so quickly under oar and current.

Medea does not call to Hekate. She won't spend her last moments speaking blank words into air. She waits at the remains of her brother and watches those tiny boats gain shape and size and sees how many oarsmen, hundreds. Faceless, nameless. What is it in men that makes it impossible for them to simply watch a ship go by? Why the constant desire to kill and dominate? Even in herself, relentless, a need to conquer. She would make all cower on the ground before her, every man in every land.

Those boats very fast, narrow and low, and the wind weak. The Argo a large pig of a boat, heavy, turning numbly this way and that, never sailing in a straight line, swept along more by current than by oars. The Argonauts tiring, slowing, looking at the Thracians. Clouds low. What Medea feels is only sadness, no excitement, no panic now but only a dull recognition of the end, unspeakably sad, the last thing any living being must feel for itself.

70

If she could go back, she would. She would make her brother whole again, breathe life into him, and obey her father. But she knows if they escape, this regret will be erased. No thought reliable, only a sign of the moment. And somewhere beneath, some churning thing that is Medea, something as unseen as what lies below these waves, and without limit or any floor that can be found.

Small bay opening to their left, and the breeze can reach their sail. Feel of that power, the hull leaning, digging in and accelerating. Jason with feet braced, lying back on deck holding that line, keeping the lower yard in place as the upper yard twists and curls.

The Argonauts on the upwind side are standing to dig their oars lower to find water. Each oar hold only by a small loop of rope shielded in hide, loose and sliding, and one man after another has to stop rowing to bend and pull more oar through the loop.

The boats of the Thracians closer now. The water unnatural, this bright blue, as if lit from below, and entirely opaque. Another headland to the left, the wind more shielded again, so the Argo wallows level. The men sit and pull for their lives.

Spearmen at the bows of the Thracian boats, braced and ready to throw. Holding round shields of hide, gray brown, in pairs like the dull eyes of oxen, without their own light. The sky a wilderness of cloud in ridges and folds heavy and shifting, coming closer, bearing down. Men as mimics only, controlled by cloud, enacting the same pressure, no different from waves on water, as relentless and inevitable and unthinking.

Gibbering among them, shouts and calls over the water, whoops, excitement of killing. Medea stays low to the deck, not wanting to offer rape as well. Shore flying by but water passing too slowly, the Argo mired again, and the Thracians gaining. Medea's life decided by something as simple as a few puffs of wind. More breeze and she lives. Less and she dies, and the Argonauts with her.

Ahead the water seems to flow to nowhere, no outlet. A long bay with walls in front and along both sides, an impossibility. River rushing into a closed canyon.

The horde coming closer, low bows slapping at the water. Oars fashioned from small trees and no more than bark removed, almost no shaping. No wide blades at the end, yet there are so many they surge forward. Undisciplined rowers looking over their shoulders at their prey.

Every fleeing ship has this one advantage, though, that its oarsmen face the stern, are looking back and can see exactly how close they are to being overtaken. Argonauts grim, pulling hard, and the gap no longer closes. Each man looking at his death from brutes wearing animal hides and shouting in a foreign tongue, death without funeral rites, far from home, ripped to pieces and thrown into the sea like Medea's brother. The golden fleece gone, voyage for nothing, names forgotten and story never told. Demigod kings hacked into meat.

Medea rises and screams, arms in the air. Enemy oarsmen pause and turn to hear what witch. She invokes the name of her father, Aeetes, son of Helios, a name they will have heard before. She promises the fleet of Colchis, a great army landing at Lygos to slaughter. She works her arms in the air as if she could bring that army now and bring also the night into the day, calls on Hekate and curses them. Your women will give birth to goats, and no Thracian will speak a human tongue.

Some among them will understand. Fishermen who have been to Colchis. She screams again the name of her father, her own name, Hekate's name, and sees them confused, paused at their oars, some of the pure pleasure of the chase and killing gone. Men in the nearest boat are calling to the other boats coming up behind. They pause, too. All are slowed and the Argo escaping.

Medea continues to scream her curses, though they won't hear her now. Her father has saved her. Thracians turned away, the difficult row upstream back to their harbor. Long boats like centipedes, so many oars, crawling into the distance.

The channel opens to the left, no dead-end canyon but a sharp bend, and this faces the Argo too close to the wind, so the Minyans have to drop the upper yard, collapse the sail. Six men to do this. Here is where they would have been overtaken if not for Medea. They owe her their lives, and she intends to make them pay.

Glare on the water ahead in this bend, all color gone. Swept by current, wind blowing against them, boat sagging toward land. No way of knowing how deep the water. Stranded on some bar in this river-sea, they'd be helpless. Small encampments along the bank, more Thracians.

Medea silent again, her hands shaking and some shaking also in her chest. More rage now than fear. What fear converts to, the desire to kill. She paces her small area of deck behind the rudder posts, a kind of cage.

Jason's men exhausted, moving numbly at the oars, but he shouts at them to row harder. The helmsmen need speed for steering. The bow swings one way and then another, and the shore comes closer.

Clouds advancing in long lines, bunched and gray, heavy. No part of this world still.

The channel bends to the right, easier, straightening out, the downwind shore no longer a threat, and the men haul the yard again, sail billowing out over the right side of the boat. The Argo tipped and sliding along, its bow held to the left in order to go straight, moving like a crab.

Small encampments all along the Thracian shore but nothing like Lygos, no boats pursuing. The other shore strangely vacant. Such an important passage, and no one here. The Hittites not ranging this far. How each people came to a certain place and not another. Histories forgotten, all in every land believing in their own inevitability, that they somehow were born of a place and always meant only for that place. Yet someone will live on this shore someday and they aren't here now.

The world is too big. Who can say how far the empty lands and seas extend? In almost any direction you might walk the rest of your life and find no one. Desolate places home only to gods, or the desire for gods, great behemoths churning through land and sea and air to keep all from dissolving into nothing. Oceans risen into vapor and swept away, entire mountain ranges collapsed into dust and forgotten, if not for the gods. This is what they do, holding together the unseen world, preserving. This is why they exist and why we can never find them. Once we arrive in a place, they leave, their work done.

The Argonauts resting now. Oars shipped and sailing. Pursuers unseen waiting anywhere ahead, so they'll need their strength then. Drifting an impossible current draining nowhere, and Medea thinks they must have lied about passing this way before. She can't imagine they could have rowed against this current.

Perhaps if they had anchored along the way. Fighting for a few hours then anchoring again. It might have been possible, some tremendous and unstoppable will, clawing their way along, dreaming of gold, fearing those mythical rocks that could appear at any moment to grind them to dust, great boulders rising from the sea. A story she'll no longer be able to imagine after gazing at this calm water, almost no waves, sheltered river without rocks at all.

Ship of sleep swept along quietly in a breeze, roll of the hull and creaking, tug of the sail. Small birds landing on the yards. Impossible to believe what happened before. The past always like that, shrunken and undone and unlikely.

Sea road made by unknown hands, the Argo ushered on its course, effortless. Small coves and headlands passing until the mouth opens into another sea and there is no sinkhole, no fall into an abyss but only the water slowed and current disappearing without pull, unclear what had ever tugged at it, some rift unseen. The Argo slowed, having to make its own way again, blunt bowed and lazy.

The men not returning to the oars. Jason allowing the slow progress of the sail, the sun breaking through overhead, clouds dissipating. Day long and air hot and thick. Heading toward some distant shore unnamed.

Time. Never steady. Always quickening or slowing. A day can be of any length, and a ship drifting through an open sea makes the longest day.

One of the men sings. A voice that seems to come from farther over the water, not originating here. Mournful song. She thinks he must be missing someone. Argonauts only a band of men, without name, as inanimate as wood, until one reveals himself like this. The fisherman and now the singer, missing some woman, perhaps, wanting to be somewhere else, opening of a life. His eyes closed and head fallen back, face tilted toward the sky. Alone and every other man made alone, and Medea, too. The men will not look at each other, each traveling singly into another time. Hollow voice, low and lost, rising in desire and falling again. The world collapsing all around them, far places brought close.

Every life short and also endless, and song a way back, wandering. His face almost flat, darkened mask, but that mouth, caving. Medea closes her own eyes, sees willows along the river, summer heat and shade but then winter and the making of bread, her nurse, a man whipped, the forest when she was older and then, falling back, her young brother, lying on the bank talking about a future Colchis with himself as king, fanciful visions in which he and Medea invented how all in Colchis should walk on one hand and one foot or sleep in bundles or hang upside down to eat and drink. Their sister Chalciope saying their father would be king forever, no future king. Every time in memory living inside every other, with no separation, no distance between, and Medea doesn't understand how this can be, how all can collapse. A voyage at sea nothing by comparison, no distance traveled at all.

Day in which all are lost, even after the song's end. A far shore appearing, and after sunfall they drop the sail, anchor and go ashore for the night.

Small fire, no bodies covered in oil, no shouting or loud songs. A simple meal of fish and water and the men exhausted still, disappearing into the forest to sleep, souls around a fire vanishing one by one. The wind no more than a murmur in the pines, the air warm.

Medea follows Jason into the trees, where he lays hides on pine straw and they move slowly and she feels a tenderness for him, wanting to hold his face in her hands. The night seems perfect to her, and she does not feel alone. As he falls into sleep, she lies on his chest and feels her love for him. Some softness inside her, as foreign as this place.

She wakes in fright. A man screaming, one of the Argonauts close to the fire, a spear driven through him. Bare
chested and this wooden shaft coming out of his belly, unnatural grafting. Disbelief, his hands pulling as if the roots might
be dislodged. Struggling on his knees in the dirt, oblivious to
foreign men standing above. A club swung high and brought
down on his shoulder, sickening thud, crushing of bone. Face
rolling to the side, and he seems without air, and the club
comes down again on his head and he falls.

Other screams now, all through the forest, shouts and
grunts and knocking of shields.

Jason rising with his spear, attackers everywhere. Medea expects to see her father, golden mask and feathers in fire-light, but these are other men. Not Colchians, not Thracians, not Hittites, but a people she's never seen before, hidden along these shores, nameless. Wearing animal hides on their heads, as if they could invoke beasts.

Jason without his shield. She grabs it quickly, heavier than she had imagined, rough wood and hide, and runs after him, but the trees are filled with bodies, glint everywhere of fire on skin and spear point, and she's lost him. She has no weapon other than this shield, so she slams an edge into the back of a man's neck, where hide drapes onto his shoulders, and he staggers, turning toward her, and an Argonaut drives a spear into his side.

It's not the man impaled who screams this time. It's the Argonaut, his face twisted and terrified, howling for blood, ramming the shaft deeper. Every man gone mad. Medea so terrified she screams also, as high and frightening as she can, calling on Hekate. She swings her shield into the back of a man's knee and he folds but swings a club as he falls. She catches it on the shield and is thrown by the impact.

Bodies too soft for this. Mashing sounds and spray of flesh, the air wet, raining blood.

She tries to hide, tries to find Argonauts. They seem to be gathering at the fire, backs to the flame. The bear-man swinging his war hammer, huge hunk of bronze at the end, crushing bodies. She runs in beside him, holds her shield as defense for his side, and sees Jason. He's chopping with a short ax, chopping off a man's arm at the shoulder, something white showing, not bone but something else. The man looking down at his shoulder and oddly calm, no longer fighting, just standing there. He's covered in blood and seems fine. Then Jason chops at his neck and the blade catches, snags, and Jason is yanking to free it, the man shaken into a kind of dance. Eyes looking upward and mouth open, finding some new god, given over, priest and sacrificial victim, presiding at his own death.

Medea near the flames, this man and all others flickering presences with no single shape but shifting, leering closer and vanishing and appearing again, enormous and shrunken. The man won't fall, remains on his feet as he's shaken. There could be no end to this odd dance, so Jason lets go and the man turns and totters off toward his own people.

Smell of blood and viscera. A man smashed in his midsection by the war hammer, burst and flattened unnaturally, crawling away.

Some gathering, a surge. A dozen men charge, led by their king in a golden helmet. For a moment Medea thinks it is her father after all, but the mask is different, the body younger, as if her father could go back in time. This other sun king leaps toward the bear-man and is caught on a spear, lifted, dangling in the air for a moment, impossible shape, Jason knelt on the ground at the shaft. A king in flight, rising in a small arc like a minor sun, then collapsing to the ground, mask fallen away.

Jason yells. Cyzicus. A name. He yells it again, and all men stop. I am Jason of Iolcus, he shouts.

All men come closer, gathering around the fallen king. Jason become his nursemaid, kneeling at his side, and it's clear they were friends. A mistaken attack.

Lament. Groans and rising into more, into howls, Jason more distraught than any other. Weeping and sounds up high as if there were women here, all spears and shields dropped to the ground, every man on his knees. So strange, that slaughter is fine as long as the men haven't met before.

Medea not mourning with the others. Still crouched by the fire behind her shield, wondering at the stupidity of men, outraged. But she holds herself back, says nothing, does nothing. Even she knows not to interfere at the death of a king.

They need to remove the spear, but they don't want to hurt the body. Weeping and arguing at the same time, turning his body on its side and working the shaft through, twisting and trying not to harm, but some of the men seem to think he might still be alive. Impossible, with a spear through his chest and all his blood gone, bone crushed, but they hate that there should be any discomfort. Other men groaning in the dust and pine needles, bleeding and dying, and no one helps them, because they aren't kings. The one with his midsection smashed and leaking still crawls toward some unnamed destination farther out in the trees, some fountain or spring perhaps, some rumored well. Who can say what the mind becomes when the body is crushed and maimed and lost? The dancer with the ax in his neck has wandered off to his own promised place.

The dead are too far, and how we cross over none can say. Is the dancer or the crawler any closer?

Hekate. She presides over all of this, over death and dying and darkness and the mind entering that darkness, and Medea is her priestess and knows nothing. All we would want to know opaque. All we can retreat to is an older god, to Nute, and because we are unable to reach darkness, we use a woman's form, let night live inside her so that it will be contained, and let her give birth to the sun each day. We would swallow night and death and refuse both. And before Nute? Only terror, if there was any mind at all.

These men yank at their own hair in order to control. They would have a say in death. They would accompany the fallen and keep watch during the journey.

When the spear has been removed, Cyzicus is lifted by six of his men, with Jason cradling the head. They walk into the trees guided by torchbearers who have taken from the fire, followed by mourners who beat their own faces and tear their own hair. A few men help the wounded and dying now, lift them to their feet, but almost all who are wounded want to stay curled and close to the earth, scream out in agony as they're lifted and stretched. Death pulling from underground, some current irresistible, some comfort to darkness, to a return.

The dead are carried away too, or dragged on their backs with arms outflung, as if they would hold all the sky at once. Bodies moving numbly in shadow until the grove has been emptied and there is only the fire and Medea and small waves breaking on the shore, the Argo spinning idly at anchor.

She must follow, but she would rather stay. She doesn't wish to mourn a king stupid enough to attack his friends, stupid enough to rush a spear. She doesn't wish to mourn any king. Let them all die right now, fall to the ground and never rise again. And the mourning will be endless, with feasts and games and unbearably long speeches, every woman looking at her wanting to slit her throat. The men untouchable, blameless, but not a woman.

These nonpeople, whose name has extended nowhere, led by a king too young. Let them all vanish from the earth and never have been. Her father is coming. His ship could be passing into this smaller sea right now, sailing through night toward this shore, following the wind the same as the Argo. Thieves forgetting to run. The wind is holding, and they should be using it.

City of fire. An entire hillside of torches, every woman awake and waiting for the return of her husband or son. Patches of flame unconnected, so each house seems to float in blackness, as if this hill were a wave risen up and all this light revealed within.

Unnatural, all that is human. Living with fire, turning a hill into a city, sailing over the sea, killing for no reason. This place carved from the night and separated from earth and sky.

Medea stops in darkness, alone, and wants never to enter a city again. She closes her eyes, listens to the thrum of cicadas, the air warm.

Then she hears the wailing of women, a great din from across that hillside, their king dead, their men slaughtered. Predictable, wailing exactly as they would, yet they go to war over and over, endlessly.

Medea walks on, sees the procession up the hill and torches come close together, as if all the stars in a wave could gather, the same as when she swam at night, exactly the same. Very strange the world can repeat itself in this way, in the sky and in the sea and on a hill at night, all essentially liquid and changing. Even the unnatural works of humans are repetitions and mirrors, made natural again, no different from stars submerged.

What she wants is to find herself at the center of what makes all liquid and changeable. She would add her will to what controls these shifts. She would see that lights on this hillside might swarm as the lights in the water did below, and she would be the one to make them swarm, and she would do it only because the repetition is beautiful, because form mirrored is form recognized. Instead of mourning the death of a king, she would see pattern in kings and people and bring the death of a king whenever needed and only if he offered some symmetry. The death of this king beautiful because he was slain by his friend, because the attack was a mistake, made at night, and echoes all that humans do in darkness, all the turns they take in their lives, always blind. His story will be useful to a hundred generations to follow.

What Medea doesn't know, of course, is how to come any closer. Where the symmetries are held none can say. A priestess should know, but Medea is sure that no priestess knows. She is sure no priestess is greater, no seer or oracle clearer sighted. If any of this will be found, it will be found by her. Another reason she left Colchis, to move more freely, to no longer be constrained.

At the top of the hill, a small citadel of stone, a fifth as large as her father's but larger than she would have thought for a nameless people. The king's wife will come down and weep and wail, and his children if he has any. Medea would like to see this, to judge how well the queen grieves, so she hurries toward the gates, which are only a gap in a low wall, abandoned, a torch to either side. Any army could walk through right now. Everyone in the city gone to the citadel.

A street of mud and shit, dug by the hooves of animals wandering freely, Medea's feet sinking into the mire. As if there were no stone available. A lazy, disgusting people. Mud hovels woven with sticks, the smell of human shit also. Yards of shadow, only a few torches remaining along the road, all light gathered above, and the only souls left the old and infirm, sat and gazing dumbly into nothing.

Higher on the hill, the road turns to stone. Medea wipes her sandals on the edge, but the filth is all the way past her ankles. She'll have to wade into the sea.

New shrieks above, more urgent and terrified, but not the shrieks of a single woman, the queen. Instead, this is many voices and spreading. Some new thing has happened. Medea fears for Jason, alone at the head of that procession. She runs, and hears her own blood.

A crowd all moving into the citadel, bodies packed. Too small here, loose walls of stone with narrow entrances and passageways, a maze, no towering citadel above but lost as she gets close. Directionless and maddening. Smoke of torches, the walls moved by flame, seeming to shift as shadows within them hunch and resettle.

Pushing through bodies filthy and bare, reek of urine and sweat and smoke. Disgorged into a courtyard just as crowded, and she sees Argonauts. Every person here looking toward a narrow flight of stone stairs just above, leading to the upper room of this low citadel. Something has happened in there.

Medea finds her way to Jason. Cyzicus lies on the ground forgotten.

His queen, Jason says. Cleite has hanged herself.

Medea laughs. It's perfect that the queen of the nothing people would hang herself. Maybe the rest will set themselves on fire now. Jason's hand over her mouth, and he forces her down to her knees. Tears on his face. He's ruined by this night. Crying over the non-king and idiot queen. But Medea will not mourn any woman stupid enough to kill herself for a husband.

She struggles to free herself, but Jason is too strong. He shakes her hard and pushes her flat to the ground, stone covered in dirt and mire.

The daughter of great Aeetes being stepped on by rabble, by people who live in shit. Held pinned to the earth like any insect. She crawls toward Cyzicus, toward where she might stand, and vows revenge. She could use her knife now, but she will wait. She will consider. Killing Jason now, she'd be killed herself, killed for a man, same as this queen. She won't die here in a nameless place and for nothing.

Just as she had felt a stronger love for Jason. And now on her hands and knees, fate of any woman who lets herself love a man.

A sea of lament, the crowd surging above, moaning and shrieking for two pieces of meat. The heat of them, all moving as one, pressed that tightly together, but she finds Cyzicus, presses against his empty chest, hardly more than a boy without his mask, frees her legs to straddle. Hands on his chest, groin against his, and she could be riding him. Medea laughs. They would be horrified. They would kill her. But they are all looking upward to see the queen brought out dead. They want to see her neck stretched, so Medea rides their dead king surrounded by all his people, some atavistic ritual in torchlight, as if all must be fucked into the other world and no other entrance, a god of lust, barbaric god from before thought, before name.

Medea yells and hoots and laughs in that night, and none can tell. Sorrow and joy the same sounds, and everyone blind in their obedience, never imagining Medea possible. No one will ever predict her.

She stands, finally, places her foot on this borehole chest and is able to see better that way, taller, stepping on their king. Her other foot on his face, sandal covered in shit. She holds onto shoulders in the crowd, sees the queen brought out, not what you'd imagine in a queen, smaller, a lump in brown linen, not wearing animal hides at least.

She steps off into the crowd as they turn to raise their king to meet his queen, not knowing he's just been with another, a final love to last into death. Cleite will have to be alone.

Wander forever, Medea says in her own tongue. Both of you, wander alone forever in the other world and never meet, and Cyzicus dream only of me. And let this city be burned and erased and forgotten.

They raise the king and bring him his queen, puppet show from the afterlife. Refusing death, demanding ritual even if they have to carry the bodies themselves and move the limbs. Cyzicus as Cleite is brought into his arms. Lovers raised higher than the crowd, become giants, her arms around his waist, neck long enough now to hook over his shoulder. Her face dangling, openmouthed, lost in some other ecstasy. A hole in his back, her love so powerful it has eaten right through him. Jason straining on tiptoe to keep Cyzicus' head from lolling.

Medea understands now this was their wedding day. A bridal dress Cleite wears, of linen brought from some better land, and a bridal wreath in her hair, and the bands at her wrists. She waited in her wedding bed as Cyzicus went to war, was left a virgin and chose to remain a virgin forever.

The death of Cyzicus not only at the hand of his friend but also on his wedding night, his bride waiting, and when she hears of his death, she tries to cross over to join him. Too beautiful not to have been planned, some irruption of gods into this common world to form a story to last not a hundred but a thousand generations.

Cleite, Medea says. Beautiful Cleite. Not some sad, small thing. Much larger than I thought. But you will still be alone. You will wander and never find him. The one he lay with first after death was me.

Medea wants all to know this last part of the story, the most beautiful and sad part that makes the rest, but of course no one will ever know. They carry the lovers now to their wedding bed, would give back what Cyzicus and Cleite have lost. Carried up the stairs holding each other close, let down gently to pass over the threshold, disappeared within to lie together. The sound could be of revelers at a wedding, not so different, a crowd weeping in joy rather than grief, the beginning rather than the end. Each part mirroring every other part, all repetition and pattern.

Small citadel and a people living the most important moment of their history. All who came before and all who will come after will be forgotten. Only this night matters.

Unremarkable sky above, stars appearing briefly then gone again, low cloud moving but no storm, nothing to mark the occasion. No howling of beasts in the wilderness around them. Gods working invisibly, mute shaping to go unnoticed,

and perhaps it has to be this way. The story has to be about
Cyzicus and Cleite and Jason and not about the gods. Cyzicus
has to be the one who chose, not sent against his will, and
Cleite has to have chosen also, when her time comes.

Small citadel, and all the rest of the world blind to what has
happened. They won't hear until later, and by then, they will
imagine something else. Cleite will have urged Cyzicus to
attack, making a fatal error, or she will have been the one to
first see smoke that evening along the coast, or Cyzicus will
have turned back but then changed his mind again and contin-
ued on. Some moment that would have changed everything.

And what will they imagine when they hear of Medea's
story? It won't be the same as with Cyzicus and Cleite. Every
woman will want to imagine herself Cleite, making that sacrifice, honored and lamented by her people. But who will
want to stand on the stern of the Argo with her own brother
chopped to pieces at her feet? Who will want to be an outcast or betrayer? It will be a different kind of story, tale of
a monster, a story of what is not human. Every king has
bathed in blood, but that is told differently. Cyzicus won't be
remembered for those he slaughtered. He'll be remembered
for the wedding night he didn't have, for the love of Cleite,
for his friendship with Jason, for his youth and bravery. Every
story born in pattern and wrought by the telling into another
pattern again.

Medea seemingly invisible in this crowd, but then she is
summoned, and the crowd parts to let her through. Daughter of a greater king. She will be used to mark this occasion.

Up the stone stairs to the home of Cyzicus and Cleite, and
Jason takes her arm at the threshold, as if his touch could be

only kindness. Not convenient at the moment to grind her into the dirt.

The room larger than she had imagined, higher ceilinged, but no rope dangling. Then she sees it, at a rafter by a window. Cleite jumped out the window for a greater fall.

She lies now in his arms, arranged on the bed. On their sides, turned and holding each other, snake-necked Cleite staring into that empty borehole of the spear shaft.

Trick of the dead, always, to seem alive still. Cleite's head ducked low and brought against his chest seems to be moving, tucking in closer, the most basic and beautiful affection. His hand on her back pulling her near. Hint of a smile on his dead lips, some contentment. Medea would not be surprised to see him kiss her forehead.

All in this room are silent and have knelt, pulled downward and falling endlessly within themselves, the dead some enormous weight that tumbles without resistance into nowhere, anchored to the living. An entire city might sink yet there would be no sound and all would seem not to have moved. Worlds within worlds. Anyone still for long enough can lose hold.

Long night, and there are no words. Only observance as Cyzicus and Cleite complete their vows. This room tilts on its side, swings back again and caves and fills. Pain in Medea's knees then lost again until the air becomes a dark dark blue, cold and paling.

Outside a moaning, low keening broken, no longer holding to disbelief. King and queen dead, wedding night gone, and each day will be lengthened, passing of the sun slowed.

Carved into a hill, ancient tombs in rock. Place of ancestors. Dried skulls within, measuring time. Royal tomb, opened now, rocks pulled away from the entrance. Cyzicus and Cleite waiting in shade, lying together under the sky one last time. A better wedding, Medea thinks. Lying there peacefully, a summer morning, yellow and white butterflies lofted and falling, suspended in nothing. No shouts or wine but only a stillness and the reassuring sound of small stones pulled away and tumbling, quiet work in a field.

More tombs opened lower on the hill for his men. Who first decided to bury here? And why bury the dead? We don't know the origins of anything we do. We might live in a place where the heads of the dead are chopped off and flung into the air again and again, passed among every person in the city, thrown twice by each pair of hands, and this would be the way things must be.

This nameless people removing stone after stone, opening the past, grown quiet, touching the sacred. Hollows never forgotten, a parallel city in which one might open her mouth to speak and all would wait centuries to hear. Imagine sitting long enough that your clothing falls away to dust.

Several Argonauts will take up residence, foreigners in the city of stillness, buried far from home, lying alongside those they've slain or who would have slain them. Some desire to reach for a spear preserved, suspended. Abandoned by Jason, who works to free the tomb of Cyzicus. Jason political, every act of his calculated, and this she must remember. No loyalty in him.

What his men think she doesn't know. They labor now at the rocks as they do at the oars, dumb as cattle, mute. She will never believe they are kings and demigods. Bare backed and burned by the sun, no better than slaves. The shadows around them shortened, the sun high overhead, and they are silvery with sweat as if spun by thread of spiders, long reaching arms only tracings in light, no sub-stance, no flesh. Bright outlines in the air, wavering in every slight breeze.

Shallow tombs, enough only to keep the dead from being eaten. When all are opened, everyone gathers, people appear-ing from the trees on all sides, brought together without signal. They speak the name of Cyzicus as he is pushed inside headfirst among the bones of his ancestors, dark place from which no one returns. Voices rising as Cleite is pushed in with him, a greater lament for the queen.

Jason standing at the entrance, first among mourners, first in worship of himself. Medea should join him, she knows, but she remains where she is, at a distance.

Every ritual should be at night, by fire. The day too solid and hard, nothing shifting or becoming, all made smaller. The Hittites burn their dead, and a king's burial lasts for thirteen days. Immolated at night for every god and dark corner of the world to see, the fire extinguished with wine. His bones oiled and wrapped in a double layer of fat, something to be devoured. To provide a rich life afterward, perhaps, but it seems also a way to call the wolves. Hellhounds of Hekate, misshapen creatures of the weather god of the sea, and every other demon waiting to tear and scatter and consume.

This burial of Cyzicus only a body placed in stone, and another body, and another, stacking of firewood. Most ancient of rites, leading all the way back before memory, simple burial in a cave. But these people have no priestess to lead them, only a few old men wearing bones and mumbling to themselves, incoherent, making nothing from nothing. An old rite become too old, gods far away and sleeping, all their good work with Cleite reduced.

Slain Argonauts placed in their foreign tombs, Jason presiding, saying a few words. Each man apparently was the finest of all men, the bravest in battle and strongest, despite being so easily killed, and each a king in some land that must overlap or expand infinitely to make room for so many kings. Minyans liars, a people of outrageous words and no particular deeds.

Heat of the day moving in, all wobbling a bit as they stand, grown dizzy and bored, wishing Jason could have fewer words. And the dead are not great performers themselves. They lie there, then are stuffed away. A stomach grumbles, a few thoughts of food.

She sees now why her father hangs the dead from trees in untanned ox hides. Grove at the edge of the city never forgotten. Spinning in the breeze, sacks of flesh in the open air. Men eternal, associated with the sky, only the women forgotten below. Over time, the city will be ringed by the dead, and none will leave or enter without passing these strange cocoons.

Her father out there somewhere still, looking for the remaining pieces of his son, unwilling to hang only part of a prince.

Unclear what gods her father worships, what gods might be angry if a sack is only half full. Helios his father, but does he believe this? The weather god of the sea, unnamed, faceless, is a god he might fear after this voyage, but Medea suspects her father believes in no gods except himself. Ox hides a barrier, perhaps, from all that would devour, some mythical power of the ox to keep hellhounds and every other creature away, but Aeetes most likely believes the air is empty, holding no form beyond what we know. This grove of the dead a monument only to his own rule, even the dead remaining his subjects.

What if all people hung their dead in trees, and not only the men but the women too? Are there enough trees in Egypt? How many have died in a land that old? Trees burdened until their limbs bend and finally are torn off and the bodies turned to mush are heard from far away as they land, soft pats on the earth, a kind of rain. Forests of the dead to cover and seed the world again.

Stones and caves a form of erasure. How deep was this cavern when it was first found or dug? The rock soft enough to enlarge. Do Cyzicus and Cleite lie on dirt and rock or on layer after layer of bones that have decayed into dirt? None here can say. Old men mumbling in conversation with nothing. All bodies disappeared and narrow entrances filled again with stones, lives sealed away and forgotten.

Sun falling through the sky in its endless succession of days, and all labor cyclical. Closing these tombs with stones only to open them later again. What Medea must do is make her life matter. Her days must be recognized and remain and not be buried and lost. How to do this unclear. Surrounded on every side by erasure.

Jason looks oiled, laboring among the stones, back rippling. Aware of being watched. Not taking water or rest. Young king in his fabled days before he was king. Stories will be told. The rock alive, and he will have torn at the mountain itself to free a proper burial place for his friend Cyzicus. Throughout this journey, giants of every kind will have fallen at his feet, giants of stone and water and sky. If enough people repeat the stories for long enough, Jason will become something that cannot die, but he also will have been erased, because the actions are too large and impersonal. The stories will reveal nothing about the real man who lived. Medea would have something more personal, something remembered and caught and frozen that can be only her, some moment none can fully understand or forget.

A feast, to remember the fallen. Goat meat cooked in blood, gruesome reminder of battle and yet none seem to notice. Pieces of liver and heart and brain bobbing with the meat in each dark bowl, as if organs could have been taken from the dead to rejuvenate the living. Some elixir to eat another man's heart or devour his brain. Egyptians remove all and pickle each as a separate dish.

Sheep slaughtered also, roasting over fires, and torches everywhere, the night a conflagration. Some refusal from deep within us. Burning all darkness away, denying death.

Wine and drunken shouting, no longer still, no longer reverent. Restarting the world after this abrupt pause.

Reclaiming all for the living. And a new king, a cousin of Cyzicus, older, presiding at the steps to his new home.

No people brave enough to live without a king. In every land Medea has heard of, there must be a king, or a queen made into a king, Hatshepsut wearing a beard. Some male figure as defense against the gods of sea and air and darkness and death. Some center. Jason at his side, and Medea, and the most important of his people. It doesn't seem that a king should be made like this. Her father Aeetes descended from Helios, all history erased. That's the true making. Descended from a god, containing the beginning and the end. Not some selection made from low necessity.

Medea hates this one more than any other, because he is nothing and has been made a king anyway. An average man, sucking at bones and eyeing young women, not talking with Jason because there's nothing to say. No vision, no plans except to fuck and try not to be killed.

We need to leave, Medea tells Jason. He's drinking and looks at her as if from underwater. My father is coming. If you stay here, you die.

Jason holding a leg bone, waving it now to indicate all who are feasting and drinking. It does seem obvious that nothing will happen until night is over and the men have slept through most of the next day. But Medea insists.

You'll lie here fat and drunken and watch his spear pushed into your chest. All for nothing, for a non-king. Medea points at the new king. It's unclear whether he understands what's being said. He shares the language of Ilium, and Medea is using a butchered blend of her language and Jason's. He looks down at his meat.

Fat smeared around his mouth, same as Jason's. Shining cave holes in torchlight, devouring. Stupid pointless feasting, boring and unbearable.

Medea stands and takes a torch. I'm going to the Argo, she says. If I have to wait, I'll burn the ship.

She uses the torch to part the crowd, steps over bodies, veers away from all who lurch and leer and yell incomprehensible things. Ritual dissolved and collapsed. Men shouting in each other's faces in different languages, understanding nothing, crazed grins that deny the dead and anything sacred. Cyzicus and Cleite buried now in stone, in silence, separated from the living, beginning the slow count of endless days and nights undistinguished. Medea is surprised to feel an overwhelming loneliness, as if she too is buried in stone and cannot be reached. Coldness without end, absence forever of warmth and light and movement.

Nothing binds her to anyone. If she dies, not one person in this world will mourn. She walks alone and invisible down that hill from stone into mire and then into forest, a shape only that passes through air and leaves no trace, seems not to touch ground.

Trees in torchlight shifting to the side, following their shadows, circling behind her, leaning in from above. Her breath held, fear immediate. Running now, and the flame a hive, angry and loud, feeding on nothing. A noise too close, hiding all that comes near. Medea runs as fast as she can, flying through that night, every slope veering and tipping and the world itself shaken by every hard footfall.

Lost and no path, only blind flight until a hill falls toward a mirror, a sea too calm to be called a sea, only a pool of dark water waiting and catching flame.

No sign of the Argo, no sign of her father. No other lights. She runs along the very edge, in sand and rock, her feet nearly in the water, where the trees won't reach her, and hopes she's going the right direction, nothing familiar, no moon to guide. Pounding along the shore.

Shadow. The Argo begins as shadow, some felt weight in darkness, some part of the mirror that won't reflect, dull surface hung in the air then warming, taking shape and color, a deep brown to match flame.

Some creature impossible, a curve suspended between water and sky, waiting. It seems she could simply walk across the water to reach it. All distance gone, and liquid become solid, light the only element. Whatever surface we can see can hold us.

But the water at her ankles now cool and refusing, and she finds the small boat they use to ferry. She's careful with the torch as she slips the oars into their loops of leather and pushes away from shore.

Unbelievable that she ran in fear. The forest at night is where she has lived all her life. It must be her father. Out there somewhere, and she can feel him coming closer. Source of fear. She knows it's time to run.

Argonauts forgetting, pausing for too long, lying drunken on a foreign hillside as if all the world is theirs. They don't understand her father and what he will do.

Gliding so smooth over the water. A sweep of the oars and then pause, and all so quiet. Breath of flame from the torch, small liquid sounds beneath, drifting backward into darkness. A world held perfectly level, Medea suspended at the margin. All below and all above held in their place, all without disruption.

She would rather be this. She would bring all together, in balance and quiet. Rule without sound, without rough movement. All held and caught and perfect.

But she knows she is meant to destroy, and she knows she is not done. Pelias will be next, and if she were to stay here, she would destroy the new king, simply because his existence is a kind of insult. Where does this originate in her? Why can't she rest?

Born of no mother, so perhaps she was forged. Some other metal lighter than copper and more liquid than tin, fused more completely and fusing still, strange element that never cools, some molten core and veins tracing shape and pattern from nothing, form from darkness and some intent that can be only the nature of the material itself, inseparable and without location, no less elemental. Born to destroy kings, born to reshape the world, born to horrify and break and remake, born to endure and never be erased. Hekate Medea, more than god and more than woman, alive now, in the time of origin.

Medea alone on the Argo, old sagging ship hunched and listing, settled into the sea. Foul smell of her brother, overpowering in the still air. She stands above him at the stern, torch in hand.

Dark and fused into wood, moist growth seeping beneath what has dried and hardened. Pieces of him that found no use, her father's ship gone for too long, and difficult to believe her father would recognize the shapes now.

She sets the torch in the bindings of a rudder, kneels and uses a long wooden spoon from the cookery to sever the largest piece from the deck. Pushing in between wood and flesh trying to free what might have been his chest. Somewhere in there, a rotted heart liquefied. The spoon emerging shiny with drool, and the smell too much. Medea retching over the side and returning to her work. Taste of bile.

A creature grown to the wood, tentacles suctioned. She has to yank upward with both hands and the spoon slips and she feels spray on her face.

She tries not to breathe. Stabs the spoon in along every edge, pries upward and hears sucking sounds of her brother releasing his hold. Rib cage flexing. She levers the spoon beneath while grabbing his shoulder with her other hand, peels him back, finally, and is able to roll him overboard. Heavy splash and a few drips and ripples extending in firelight.

Other misshapen lumps adhered to the wood, and Medea works at each of them, delivers this meal to the depths. Who knows what feeds below, some scent in darkness and the will to devour. She scrapes and pries until every last piece of her brother is gone, then she dips a length of linen into the sea and uses it to scrub at the deck, dips it again and again until the wood is almost smooth, wrings out the last of him and stands breathing hard in the night.

No movement, no sound, as if nothing lives beneath the surface and even the winds will never return. Still air, warm and without shape, her torch long since died out, gone mute. Only the smell of it and the smell of rot and the smell of the sea. The Argo as unmoving as land.

Medea goes forward and lies on deck just ahead of the mast, curls on her side to wait. Womb inside womb, the Argo, the sea, this night, and whatever encloses the night.

She wants to sleep, but too much is uncertain. Where her father is now, whether he will find them, where they will sail, what Iolcus will be, what Jason will be, what she will be. Pelias and the long succession of kings in every land. Her home that she'll never see again, the mountains and rivers and temple to Hekate left empty.

The golden fleece stretched directly above her along the lower yard, shedding its gold onto her now, sifting through darkness like a sky fallen and falling still. Fleece that is nothing. Her father would have let them go if not for his son.

She did not need to kill her brother, perhaps. Difficult to know. We can never see the other path.

She's awakened by shouts from shore, Jason and his drunkards. They want the small boat to ferry. She sits up and sees flame, all their torches lighting the trees above like a low sky that follows, pulsing. They stand at the edge of reflection in this narrow band between water and heavens, giants seen from far away but behaving like children, petulant cries. Smooth mirror and they could be caught here forever, but then Jason wades in, disrupting the surface, creating a wake and sinking until he's only dark movement without feature.

Medea lies back down, last moments of rest before she'll be trapped again on the stern. Sound of the small boat knocking against the side as Jason climbs in. Splashing and struggle, then calm sound of oars, regular and fading. The Argo rocking gently.

The men come aboard stinking of sweat and smoke, animal fat and wine. Stumbling and slow, lying in heaps on the deck, useless crew. She retreats behind the rudder posts to avoid being stepped on.

Torches everywhere. They may burn the ship down themselves, flames dangerously close to the lower yard and sail.

Cursing as they haul meat and water and wine, all in an ugly mood. Demigod complaints.

Endless trips rowing back and forth, the small boat never going straight, slow arcs and corrections, and by the time they've finished and are pulling this boat onto the deck, the sky has paled and the sea become opaque light blue.

Flat calm, all waters extending as one, reaching all the way to Colchis and Iolcus and beyond, filling every hollow in the land and seeming to rise, a slow swelling. Their own ripples soft and fading. Medea could live on the sea. More alive than any forest.

Some thrill to setting out as they raise the anchor stone and take to the oars. A half crew only, the rest lying on deck, but some deep pleasure in gliding across that calm. Medea at the stern looking back toward the light. The smallest of wakes, no more than a seam, and small whirlpools evenly spaced to either side where each oar has dipped, silent vortices spinning themselves out and vanishing.

Hills behind outlined and gaining weight, hills that will never be seen again, every voyage a constant receding of anything familiar, and this is at least half the pleasure. Not only what will be but also the leaving behind of all that was.

If she had been allowed, if women had been allowed, she would have been a sailor. By now she would have visited Egypt and every other land. Purest form of freedom.

Low song from the men as they row, because they're still drunk. Moving easily at the oars, second nature. Some with their eyes closed. Wearing odd bits of animal hides given to them, bracelets of bronze. Like priests at a temple, bending and moaning and bending again, hunching in unison to a quieter god, transported over the surface as if all waters were made for this.

There must be at least one god not filled with rage. Medea closes her eyes and tries to remember, but every image, every name that comes is feared. She hasn't understood this until now, that rage is god, every weather god, every elemental, all that rise from the earth, all that come from death, all with a will to destroy. Worship a form of fear and perhaps nothing more, but how can that be?

She tries to imagine the quiet god, the god unfeared, without rage, who will not destroy. The god who does not demand to be obeyed, who threatens nothing, some god who would have all sleep and eat and glide across calm water and be content, but this erases all human form. This god would have to take the form of a tree, or grass, or some flower, something without voice or thought or will. Rage that inescapable and human.

The Argo slips toward the strait at Ilium, where her father could be waiting. No other boats or sign of people along the shore, no wind, and so it seems the world might be new, not yet populated, the winds not yet begun. The one god of peace not yet given birth to lesser gods who would stir the air and lash the seas and tear up the earth, not yet released havoc.

Argonauts hunched at the oars half sleeping, throwing off animal hides as the air heats. The sky cleared, clouds gone, and a faint breeze begins. Water etched in dark patterns, the mirror gone.

A small fishing boat, and another, and all is slowly built. Huts along the shore, ripples on the water, more men at the oars, Jason looking at the sail, considering. Medea looks everywhere for her father, feels always that he must be near.

A large island ahead on the right, narrow passage between it and shore, and several small protected bays, coves perfect for hiding a ship. Jason alert, and his men, also, looking over their shoulders now.

The wind rising, small waves, and they would use the sail if the passage ahead weren't so narrow. Trapped and funneled toward whatever awaits.

Jason climbs the yards, stands just above the golden fleece, holding onto the mast. The ship swaying. He's searching for the mast of her father's ship, a slim dark line that might be waiting in any cove. Young and muscled and false, not to be trusted, but he is beautiful and he is all she has.

No one looks at her. Not Jason or any of his men. Since they've come on board, not even a glance. She inhabits some vacant place in the air. Each man at the oars somehow managing to never look straight ahead as he rows. A strange art to this, drawn to deck and water and sky and nowhere.

So she opens the deck, crawls below and decides she doesn't care whether her father is waiting along this coast. The hold filled with wine and water and meat and several new fishing nets. She has to push her way through in narrow bands of light from the seams above to reach the rudder posts and the rope coiled there, her bed. The only safe place. She falls easily into sleep, wakes at the sound of the anchor line running over the side, falls asleep again and wakes in the night.

Gentle rocking of the hull, and she waits and listens but hears nothing except the soft creaking of wood and rope. She crawls in darkness through spaces too narrow, panicking a bit, pushing at deck overhead that won't open, buried. She thinks for a moment the crew could have placed a weight on the hatch to keep her trapped, but then she finds the piece of deck that lifts free.

Released, she stands in that night the only soul awake. They've posted no sentry. All sleeping and hoping to be killed. Small cove, a light breeze, the Argo hung at anchor. Protected cove in a protected channel. Darkness of the land, a deeper shadow surrounding.

The Argo too small. She strips and goes over the side, into cool water, swims toward the front of the ship and past its anchor line and keeps going into the channel. Away from land. She doesn't know how deep it might be here, or what might be waiting below, and this is what she wants, to hang at the top of the world as larger creatures pass beneath, great behemoths that live always in darkness, because she has this same feeling on land, that something always is working below us, movement unseen and waiting, enormity that cannot be known or controlled. Some relief in challenging this directly, waiting here to see whether she'll be devoured. Eyes covered in white, opaque, teeth curled, breathing water and cold and knowing, somehow, exactly where she is. She does believe that everything below knows she is here.

Medea lies back in the water, floating suspended, looking up into stars. No moon, and this thick, heavy braid across the sky, a kind of cloud more distant, made of pinpoints of light too numerous to be counted. Impossible to reach, impossible to explain, how they hang there, why they give off no heat, how they move or don't move, how large they might be.

Her arms in the water giving off no correspondent light, no longer any stars below, an occasional hint and nothing more, and this too is impossible to explain, why the liquid stars can be found one time and not another.

What she knows is only that the sea at night is the truest of temples, where all is offered. The Argo no longer close. No safety. She swims farther away, midchannel, hangs suspended over all that can be imagined and cannot be imagined. She offers herself, to be devoured or saved, and all is borrowed. The heat in her body fading, the effort to stay afloat, the precious air. Temple where none can remain.

Her temple to Hekate on land was nothing, she sees now. She might have fallen asleep there one night, slept for years and awakened to find nothing changed. Simple stone, cold and unreachable. She could have shat on the floor and scattered every fire and thrown wine and all would still have been mute. The blood of animals wasted. Only here in the sea is something wagered. Here she offers everything and everything can be taken and nothing remains the same. Every wave and ripple new, every movement below, and blood offered now would bring every tooth near. Blood offered now could not be survived.

Hekate, Medea says. Hekate no less than this sea and all that connects to this sea, and the night above. I'm sorry I thought you smaller. I never will again, and there will be no temple, only coming to you in the night like this.

Heat fading, legs kicking below, arms become tired. Medea remains as long as she can, looking up into that thick braid, but finally swims back toward the Argo. A shadow lost against shadows beyond, but she knows where it will be, and as she comes close, its bow rises against the stars.

Sleeping crew, all unaware, resting on this thin curve of wood. Exhausted and spent and surrendered, and where her father has gone, none can say. Difficult to believe he exists. Some phantom fear, fabricated.

Medea pulls herself up the ropes over the side and stands naked on deck, her skin tight and cold. Drapes linen warm but dirty, smelling of too long on this boat and also of fires on shore. Living like an animal here. How long until they reach Iolcus? She wraps herself and lies in the burial place on the stern, looks up at stars until her eyes close and she's gone again.

A following sea and the sail raised, perfect breeze, some sign of favor. They clear the islands with no sign of her father, enter open water again but the shores narrow ahead, funneling toward the second strait, last place he could be waiting.

Brown linen sail curved and straining, rippling then taut again, capable of infinite shapes. Hunching to one side and then another, revealing the air. Medea feeling some similar tug, lying on deck and staring until there is only the sail and the sky and no longer any feeling of a ship or the sea. Pulled upward and she can't say which is closer: the sail might be recessed far away, the sky nearer. It flows off the edges and falls closer but never reaches her, endless movement which is no movement at all.

The sail no inanimate thing. Terrible in high wind, rigid and merciless and powerful beyond imagining, a thing of fear and will. But even now, in lighter winds, filled with desire, a restlessness, capable even of regret and sorrow, falling along an edge, hunching down, refilling but not entirely, some cost to the past. Only in no air, when it hangs fully slack, does it seem like linen. At all other times, this is impossible to believe.

The sail not a god itself but only the tracing of a god, a more responsive form of temple. Like fire to reveal Hekate. How can we know when we're worshipping a god and when we're worshipping only the sign of a god? Wind itself a sign of something else, and even fire, and what hides behind them? The world built in too many layers, a suffocation, all gone mute, sources lost. All we can worship are shadows.

The shores remain far away, low mountains with patches of brown, becoming drier. She's heard that all will be drier in the next sea, Helios somehow closer in his passing. And she's heard this strait is very long and pinches close at Ilium, but the shores are so far apart now it's hard to believe it's a strait at all. It looks only like a sea.

Sound of the wake, rudders in a stream, and waves building, the upwind blade rising free and plunging again, eager, like some fish made of wood, narrow headed and tireless. Whorls of air caught, twisting like strands of web. Surface flattened and smoothed by the hull, water brightened, aerated, the sound of it a thousand sounds at once, the air become liquid as liquid becomes air.

Argonauts resting behind her uninterested, never looking
over the side but only at land in the distance, oars shipped,
letting the sail work. Thinking of going ashore and drinking
wine, waiting only for wine, so why come on this venture at
all? Why not stay at home in a pile and pass out?

Fame, probably, each dreaming of his name sung forever,
not realizing no one can remember even four generations
back. Almost everyone erased within three generations. Jason
may be remembered, but not his men. The list of his crew
will never be certain. Demigods in their own lifetimes only,
then misremembered shadows, misshapen, then forgotten
entirely. Nothing, as if they had never been born. Or worse,
become only a name, with nothing left attached.

Floating over these waves unnoticed, unrecognized, insignificant. Jason far away at the bow, resting there, looking
back at her, thinking what? He chose her, and she chose him,
unthinking, in an instant. Some tie they can't see that binds
them nonetheless.

Medea walks forward, every sailor moving away slightly
as she passes, walks beneath the fleece that bows out like the
sail and still shimmers, not yet lost all its gold, and stands
before Jason.

Are you finished pushing me into the dirt? she asks.

Yes.

His face sincere, no king but only a boy. She sits on deck
and leans back against him. His arms around her, and she
closes her eyes and does not feel alone. So much must be
ignored and erased for her to be here, but she's willing to
do this: some basic animal need, to be held, to spend each
night and even the day next to another body. She knows

the sailors are watching, knows they think her weaker now, the stories no longer only of fear, but there will still be fear enough.

Held, surrounded, by Jason and the Argo and the sea, listening to the sail and water for the rest of that long day, remembering her younger sister Chalciope and how they lay together most nights for years, as natural as breathing, yet became two different people entirely. Chalciope more foreign to Medea than these Argonauts. Familiar in every way, of course, in her habits and body. The weight of her arm across Medea's back, scent of her hair. But what Chalciope thought or felt Medea was never able to guess, and Chalciope would never tell. When she was old enough, she lay with their father. Suddenly gone, never to spend another night with Medea again, and never to utter a word of what happened. Content and mute and blank, as difficult to reach as the sky. Always at the side of her father, inseparable. He may have returned to her now. That could be why there is no sign of his ship. Tired of a pointless chase and returning to his other daughter's bed. But Medea doesn't really believe this. Nothing will make him stop.

When evening comes, they rise and look carefully at the land now closer on both sides, narrowing. Low hills abandoned at first, the sun buried beyond, then a few fires appearing. Long channel. It seems the Argonauts do not plan to anchor or go ashore.

Ilium, Jason says. Your father could be at Ilium or could have sent riders.

They will sail or row through the night, dangerous. If the channel bends, will they know?

Entering another strange river without fall, another current without source, sped along by something unseen. The wind dying, sail collapsing. Filling again but without power, then curling and hanging uncertain until the men lower the yard.

Returning to the oars as the last light in the sky fades, the water ahead holding that light, a final mirror, deep blue. Jason and the helmsmen lining up in the middle of the wide channel hoping it remains wide, trying to memorize the shore.

Some crossing into another world, to row blind into darkness and steer without reference. Shape of a life. Riding a current unknown.

Outline of Argonauts even when all light is gone, a sense of shadow moving in unison at the oars. Shore passing invisibly, stars appeared above but without light, too far away. Medea on the stern again, behind the helmsmen and Jason, and when she blinks, every shadow relocates, the mass of oarsmen mutable.

They could be passing her father's ship right now and he wouldn't know. A good plan. She hopes the night will hold until they've entered that larger sea.

Small fires appear along the shore on the left, though none can say for certain where the margin lies. The fires could be far back from the water. Too small to illuminate anything surrounding, and no sense of distance.

The shore on the right without fire or settlement, lost in the black. They could crash into land at any moment, wood breaking on rocks.

They row for hours, long wide channel endless, passage through Nute, and it seems possible the day might never come again. Swallowed and no rebirth, held in this night. Stars above embedded in her flesh, lit only to remind that all is enclosed, that there is a roof to the world. One vein in a body larger than imagining, lost in the vastness of this small nowhere.

Nute, Medea says. Largest god, final and first.

Jason and his men unaware of passing through Nute, unaware there may be no rebirth, that night may extend forever and this channel never end.

Fires more numerous, and these, too, like the stars above, must be embedded along the margins to show passage, a gift from Nute. Darkness unmarked would be too much. Fires even along the darker shore.

Ilium in doubt only before it's been seen. Vast glow and flames beyond counting. This vein bending to the left, narrowing, seeming almost to end, pinched close and so brightly lit even in the middle of night. Other ships moored along the edge.

Jason speaking softly but pushing his men to row faster, to keep steerage as the current strengthens, a kind of river even faster than the one from her father's sea. The Argo sliding sideways, then straight, then drifting again. Argonauts visible now in glimpses, faces lit by the glow. The water made of pale gold.

Stone walls lit by torch, a large citadel well defended. Encampments extending to every hill beyond, not as large as Hattusa but larger than her father's city. Controlling this passage between seas, gateway where the land hooks, the channel bent and narrowed.

Medea is sure they will be stopped by other ships. They reach the bend and row furiously, current sweeping them sideways. Jason encouraging his men.

City of stone among outcrops of rock the same color. Formed rather than built, emerged from the earth long before any human hands could have shaped it, mythic city raised by giants or even earlier. It may appear only in torchlight, at night. It may wink out and disappear during the day, then grow again out of darkness.

Spearmen standing along the walls unmoving, thin sentinels not yet awakened, the Argo insignificant, not recognized as a threat, drifting along out of control, oars reaching into water with little hold.

No pursuers. The city passing lit and impossible, receding quickly, already becoming rumor. The shores ahead with few fires, the channel straightening again, and their passage through Nute continues.

There is a time when nothing is in sight, when there are no fires and no shore and even the stars have vanished behind cloud. Rowing into absolute black without belief, waiting for rocks to tear the hull.

Each man alone, and Medea. No instructions to the helmsmen. They plot their own course out of nothing, try not to plot any course at all but only let the rudders run, some earlier belief that a blade of wood in water will find its way, eager for the open sea.

Medea can't see Jason, doesn't know whether he has joined the oarsmen or is on the bow looking ahead into the void for some sign, or standing on the yards.

Every sound close, magnified. Each oar dropping into water, creaking of wood and line, breathing of the men, the stream broken by each rudder. Medea strains to hear sounds beyond this, sounds to indicate larger shapes of water and land, but the rest of the world is silent. They can hear only themselves, Argo and the Argonauts and Medea in an oblivion.

The ship rolling just slightly, and no way of knowing whether they've come upright. No reference. The passages in Nute unmarked. Bends and turns unrecorded, unnoticed. Passing of all souls, each alone yet riding this same current, passing the same landmarks unseen.

Nute without heartbeat, without pulse. There should be some slow and heavy surge, rhythmic and reassuring, some giant heart hung far away above and worshipped like the sun, every ear listening in that direction, a way of measuring distance. All travelers swallowed and approaching, shaken as they come alongside, receding until just as the beat becomes indistinguishable from one's own heart the new day is born and the sun worshipped instead. Each day Nute forgotten, and each night remembered.

But Nute is never heard. There is no pulse, nothing to follow, no way of measuring distance or where one might be in that long passage. Nute refusing human form. We can imagine a woman's body, but this is only imagining.

Our own shape tries to form in darkness, something more of threat than promise but desired anyway. Something just beyond the limits of our skin, trying to solidify in the air but still shifting. Something that might fold into another and form in unison, some belief in night that we are not so separate, not held to the outlines of our own bodies.

Dream that cools as the sky blues and the first outlines become rigid, of mast and yards and water and men. Emerging from Nute, but no sense ever of the final part of that passage, because the moment day is noticed, it's already arrived. The barest hint of light, and night is over. Nute vanished before we know we've left her.

The water seeming brighter than the sky, as if it were the source of light. Wide channel, widening still into the greater sea. Calm and mirroring, long thin tracks of seabirds. No sign of her father's ship, and now she'll never know what became of him. She had expected to meet him here or at Ilium. The Argo will vanish into these islands and a larger world, unreachable.

They must have passed him in darkness. It's the only explanation, because he would have pursued, and they were delayed so long with Cyzicus he must have gone ahead. He wasn't waiting at Ilium, so he had to have been anchored somewhere else in the channel, not expecting them to row through the night.

Medea searches the waters behind, keeps expecting to see a mast or wake, but all is calm. Hekate, she calls out, loud enough for the men to hear. You have protected us in night. Medea chants to Hekate, low and soft, claiming safe passage so the men will know, but she thinks only of Nute.

The men rowing for home now. Iolcus not far, perhaps no more than a few days' sail. Wives and children and land and whatever it is they do when not on a reckless voyage. Telling lies. This is what Medea imagines, each of the Argonauts sitting by a fire at night with all his kinsmen and every other man within a day's walk, every last shepherd, telling tales of great giants made of stone ripping trees from the earth and using them as clubs. Each Argonaut at the center, his shipmates no more than shadow as he throws a giant to the ground, plunges his fist and pulls a heart of blood from stone.

Each Argonaut will have been the personal guest of kings, feasted and offered land and women and goats, but each will have chosen to return, a loyalty enough to have every kinsman kissing native soil.

No one will question one hide with a bit of gold dust. No one will ask where the other gifts are from these kings, rare objects from foreign lands. In truth, only Medea has been brought back. She is the only prize. But she might say anything, so she will not be brought to these fires. She will be hoarded away in Jason's home, if he has any sort of home at all. A would-be king denied his patrimony, and to think this one golden fleece is going to change that seems like only a wish. Pelias will not go so easily.

Medea is Jason's best weapon. Alliance through her with another kingdom. That might be worth something. Heirs royal on both sides, even if Aeetes is betrayed and filled with rage now. Someday Aeetes will be gone, and when the heirs are old enough, someone else will rule Colchis, related by blood.

They row on as the day brightens and shores fall away. A few small fishing boats disappearing along the margins and otherwise alone. Wind rising as the sun passes overhead, bringing small waves from the side. The men gather at the stern and haul two heavy lines to raise the upper yard. Tilting and swinging as it goes up, slim trunk of a pine, tapered at the ends, banging, low thuds. The bronze head with its many eyes at the top of the mast is straight, and the sail hangs out to the side, so the lines are twisted and difficult to pull through. More men join, ten at each rope. Sail fat and heavy, tipping the boat and refusing to be pulled tight, so finally they give up and leave it that way, tie off the halyards.

They sleep almost instantly. They haven't eaten, but they're so exhausted from rowing through the night they don't care.

No one relieves the helmsmen. They fight against this baggy sail and track toward where the sun will set. Smaller men, both of them, not big enough for the oars. A position of shame, perhaps, on any boat. And yet every man here is a king and a demigod. That's what they claim. So there must be at least two smaller peoples somewhere, ruled by these runts.

Runt-kings, Medea says aloud.

They ignore her, of course, if they understand.

Living close to the ground, she says, hiding in the rocks. Waiting with short little spears for some shorter deer.

One of them glances back at her, unmasked hatred. So they do understand, but of course they do nothing except what they've been told, steering endlessly while the larger men sleep.

Slaves, Medea says. Runt-slaves.

The day burning, and no amount of goading will provoke a response from the little kings, so she crawls to the hatch and realizes this is what their people must do. Anyone taller than the king must crawl everywhere. An entire people on hand and knee, going out to the fields to work, dragging wine and food through mud streets, all looking down. At least two kingdoms ruled this way. Children allowed to run only until they reach a certain height. Every temple shortened, every doorway, even the day. Everyone going to sleep before the sun has fallen. Medea laughs and crawls below into shade, to her coiled rope, checks above to see if their legs come down through, not shorter but only submerged.

Sleep after a long night, a heaviness she falls into, gentle rocking of the ship. When she wakes, the anchor line is running over the side, a sound like some great snake thrashing, pinned by its head, chaotic and wild. She can see it black and thick, the snake she feared as a child and fears still, not slack and flat like others but solid, a rough sound through grass, a low growl she heard once when she almost stepped on one. Voice of a god.

Medea rises from the hatch into the last light of day, sun burning down into water. Extinguished in the sea, another sign that the sea is Nute, or a part of Nute. Flattened and darker yellow, almost orange, distorted, compressed, as if Helios is resisting, trying to remain in the sky, pulled down against his will.

The men busy in this last light, taking wine and meat to shore. Some celebration on the island they call Lemnos. Her father lost far behind, and they're free now, in no rush to return home.

No one lives on Lemnos. No goats, even. No shepherd's hut. Strange that it has a name and that anyone would know it. Not far from the Thracian shore, but they haven't bothered to settle here. Steep island, barren and dry. Rocks sharp enough to cut your feet. Very few trees, hidden away in canyons and smaller folds.

The Argonauts build a great bonfire on the shore using every spare bit of wood. Open to the sunset but hidden from her father by a small point that forms this cove.

Water shallow and a startling bright blue even as the light fades. Milky white rock cut into a thousand sharp pieces. The men bathe and heckle, splash each other and laugh. They say outrageous things about parts of their bodies.

The evening warm, a pleasant breeze, no need for a fire, but the fire is lit anyway, and large hunks of meat hung, meat turning dark, beginning to rot. Then they oil each other, great slicks in firelight, broad backs and thighs. They've already begun on the wine.

Medea sits apart along the shore, forgotten by Jason. He's swaying already from the drink, spreading oil and shouting over all the other voices shouting. Like a flock of seabirds, some rookery distorted, grown large and held to the ground.

They've made a sort of throne for Jason, a shelf cut naturally into the rock and lined now with hides. And they've brought a red mantle from the stores below deck, thick linen dyed somehow this bright shade beyond blood, edged with purple, richer and befitting a king among kings.

They buckle it around his shoulders and drape it along his arms, admire the intricate patterns, the tales of arms and men woven into the red. Medea goes over to see. Giants with one eye, hammers forging a thunderbolt, surrounded in flame. Garish works, ludicrous. A man lifting a mountain with his bare hands, while another man sings a mountain into movement. A woman carrying a shield but all the focus on her breast. Groups of men fighting among oxen, unintelligible, all history lost, and a boy throwing a spear at a large man dragging away his mother. Stories out of time, out of sequence, remnants unattached, yet the Argonauts pretend understanding. Medea backs away and lets them squabble over what nothing means.

Then a voice, high-pitched, a man pretending to be a woman, coming from a small copse of trees, a fold in the mountain just behind. The men are silenced, and out steps one of the helmsmen.

I am Hypsipyle, he says in his high voice. Queen of this island, and I have a tale you must hear.

The men shout encouragement. Hypsipyle is escorted to Jason, to kneel before him on his throne.

We are without men, she says.

The Argonauts slap at each other, naked and oiled, laughing and offering to provide men.

Our men raided the Thracians and took many things, including foreign women, and they soon forgot us. They left us to plow our fields alone.

Jason laughs, and all the Argonauts, staggering around and slipping against each other.

Come make this your land, Hypsipyle says. We have many women for every man, and you'll find that our island is deep soiled beyond any other in this sea.

A roar from the men, and now some of them are the women of this island, puckering their mouths and walking with their asses in the air.

Hypsipyle moves in closer to Jason with hands and mouth, and Jason leans back against the stone, allowing this. So Medea must watch as this runt-king Hypsipyle swallows Jason, and he knows she is watching. The helmsman gazes at her as he moves his head up and down, a perfect revenge, Medea standing alone as the women of Lemnos meet the Argonauts.

She could have her own revenge, on Jason at least. She could bend over and let every man plow, all of them oiled and ready. She could be all the women of Lemnos. But she can't imagine doing this.

So she sits at the edge along the shore and watches, feels helpless. A ritual that does not include her, and when the story is told, she'll be erased. They'll tell of Lemnos and the most beautiful city, with carved doors opened wide, and the beautiful queen Hypsipyle, distraught over Jason's leaving. After endless banquets and young girls dancing in countless numbers, all femininity will rush to the shore, begging the Argonauts not to leave.

What surprises Medea is how much it hurts to watch Jason with another. This terrible void inside her, a coldness and desolation, more than she would have guessed.

She can watch no longer, walks away along the shore into darkness with all this moaning and laughing at her back and keeps walking until she hears only the sea, small waves, reassuring, finds trees with pine straw beneath and lies down, curls on her side to sleep and forget and feel nothing.

They sail on, and Medea worries they will never reach Iolcus. She sees now that these men have no desire to return to their lives. They would take rivers into colder lands, find the far edge, circle back and visit Egypt, then continue along that desert shore. They would claim the founding of every land and people, make the world small and attach it to themselves. Tell stories of giants felled and mountains formed, rivers and springs, the shape of the land itself recording where they've been. Denying all who came before, the long dark past, and claiming origin. The end become the beginning. This voyage setting the limits of the world.

What she fears is that there's nothing for them after this. The gathering of the kings, and what will be left to do next? Only the recounting, the memory of each of these maidens detailed, sound of her voice, scent of her neck, her eyes in late sun, depth without end. Some longing for more.

As long as they voyage, they can delay desire and also death, and who they are remains. They won't see themselves shrunken. So why would they ever return?

The Argo a kind of slug, oozing along in movement so slow you wouldn't notice. The far shores of other islands not shifting perceptibly. Only if you look away and wait long enough can you glance again and notice a change. The thought of doing this for years unbearable.

Jason hiding at the bow, as far away from her as possible, but she goes to him now, demands to know where Iolcus is.

He points straight ahead. Sleepy, exhausted from his night, still wearing this ridiculous red-and-purple mantle. Oil no longer bright on his thighs but slack looking, like the side of a fish that's been in the sun, flattening, drawn inward.

How far?

Three days.

You could use the oars.

Jason looks at his men, all lying on deck, spent. The sail barely holding its shape. These men are not slaves, he finally says.

Close enough, Medea says.

No, Jason says, angry now. You don't understand anything. And I don't have to talk with you. You are a woman.

Medea laughs.

Women don't decide what we do.

Remember the scorpion? she asks. Remember our fire on the shore under the Hieros mountains?

He doesn't respond.

Can you remember the shape of things that night? Can you remember the world bending? Can you say that you know what happened to you or to your men?

Jason clearly afraid now, the anger gone.

That scorpion is still inside you. Inside your chest. If you disobey me, it will awake.

Jason puts a hand to his chest, and she smiles. You are here to obey me, she tells him quietly, so the other men won't hear. That is your role.

His hand gripping at skin under the mantle, as if he might find a claw protruding.

I won't tell you what is inside your men, she whispers.

Please, Jason says.

You can't beg the gods, she says. And you can't beg me. You do what's required. You honor the gods. And you will always be bound. You are never free.

Medea rolls her eyes back and chants to Hekate in her own tongue, sees nothing but hears Jason command his men to the oars, hears their complaints and his urgency and wood on wood, the first splashes, creaking of rope and hide in the oar loops.

She remains at the bow, guiding them, lifting her arms high and chanting. She will shorten this sea and bring Iolcus near, and whoever awaits in Iolcus she will master too. All these men at the oars, rushing though no one chases. Panic on a calm sea.

They row through the rest of that day, anchor in the lee of an island without going ashore. No bonfire on the beach.

The fisherman casts his net from the stern. Last light on smooth remnants of waves, every facet become a soft round momentary eye, blue with an orange center and then gone. Thousands of eyes appearing and vanishing, all held on the surface, nothing below, yet he pulls fish from nothing, guts them and throws back this offering.

The fish different here in this sea, longer and smaller mouthed, slim fins and tails. Oily tasting. Cooked directly over a small fire on deck, no talking among the men.

The sun and fire gone, night passing quickly from exhaustion. They raise the anchor stone early, at first light, and row again. Medea remaining on the bow, Jason back now with the helmsmen.

This sea with endless islands. She didn't know there could be so many in the world, each individual in shape and presence, waiting. You would have to visit each one. There wouldn't be any choice. If you look at something in the distance long enough, you eventually have to go there.

The mood of each island changing through the day, flattened at first, erased in white, not set in the water or air but consumed by both. Settling later, gaining shape and weight, shadow, then reflecting last light on ridgelines.

The Argo, too, shifting throughout the day, at times fat and hot, unthinking wood, at other times responsive, slim, eager through the water, light as a spear, a kind of quivering excitement as if its timbers are alive and can take in breath. The sea slipping beneath them, islands passing quickly.

They anchor two more nights. Late the next day the men begin pointing. A peninsula, and tucked inside the bay, a very small city, Iolcus. At first, Medea thinks she must be looking in the wrong place, seeing only a village somewhere near Iolcus. So much smaller than her father's city or Ilium or Hattusa, and she wonders whether all these kings rule similar settlements. Kings of nothing. This overwhelming feeling that she's made a terrible mistake, given up everything to come rule a few shepherds and fishermen. What can possibly rise from a people so small? No other city within sight. Isolated outposts, a gathering of heads of families more than a gather- ing of kings. She's amazed now they were able to build the Argo. She sees no navy, no other ships, nothing here for her father to fear. There is this one great ship and one only. The rest are fishing boats.

What she realizes is that they haven't built the Argo. This is an Egyptian ship, somehow captured or given or bought. The Argo not something these people could have built.

She looks again carefully at the wood worn smooth at the locks, walks back to the mast to see how the deck has chewed into its sides, walks back farther to see the rud- der posts worn and infirm, loose. An old ship, not new. The bow and stern platforms gone, the heavy rope that runs the length of the deck, held up by forks, gone. Crude short benches added along the sides for the oarsmen to sit. But otherwise this is the same as Egyptian ships that have come to Colchis. She has given up everything to live with scavengers.

A dry place, hillsides rocky and burned white, reddish clay showing where it's been tilled, small gardens and groves etched into the hardscrabble. Olives and figs. Stone houses clustered on the steepest slopes, a citadel above, not large. Walls close to the harbor.

Smaller huts continuing in every direction, bits of land eaten bare by goats. Hard to know how many people might live here, but a crowd come down to the shore.

The Argo barely moving at the end, because the sail is down and the men keep turning to look and wave and shout. Jason at the bow holding the golden fleece above his head in both hands, old sheep's hide shrunken in the sun, dirty brown, with very little gold dust remaining. But the sun has not yet fallen, so it must sparkle, at least, and should be enough to fool those who want to believe.

Medea on the stern, forgotten along with the helmsmen. Sluggish drift, the men skillful to slide the prow gently onto sand.

The Argonauts landed, epic voyage complete, hopping over the sides, splashing through water and laughing as they're tackled by their women and kinsmen. Everyone gathered here, except the king. Medea doesn't see anyone who could be Pelias. Waiting in the citadel above. Now that Jason has returned with the fleece, Pelias is supposed to give him the throne, but why would any king do that? He'll be thinking now of some new plan, some new test or delay or complication, he and all who depend upon him.

Wailing, screams of grief. One woman collapsing at the shore, held up by others. Her eyes closed and mouth open, some terrible utterance that won't be completed. Medea had forgotten the Argonauts who died fighting Cyzicus. Other women wailing now, and men. Shouts of anger and despair. Their loved ones gone and no sign left. No bodies returned, nothing to bury. Funerals taken away. They struggle toward the Argo, as if the bodies might be there, and are held back, thrashing in the water. Grief always this, some movement toward nothing. And others still laughing, still celebrating.

No ceremony here. Nothing to clarify. No king come down to the beach, Jason no leader to say words for the fallen. He's busy showing off the fleece. He thinks he'll be installed on the throne today.

Medea the only soul left on the Argo, watching every-thing. She would intervene, because her own fate is locked to Jason's, but it's already too late. Jason political but also too young, too pleased with himself and his fleece, too hungry to be praised and loved.

Strangely quiet that first night. Lamentation and celebration but dispersed across several hillsides, into separate
homes, as if all have returned simply from a few days of
fishing. Medea and Jason led to rooms in the lower citadel.
Stone floors, not dirt, but small and almost empty, three
chambers connected and with almost no light. Low ceilings,
filling quickly with smoke from torches.

A table in one of the rooms. Jason lays the fleece there,
unwanted, unclaimed. He sits on a bench, his back against
the wall, and stares at the ceiling. Quiet in here, bare sound
of flame and nothing more. Wearing his red mantle still.

Medea sits on a low bench along the opposite wall, not far away, and watches him. His chest rising, slow exhales. His head slipping back, mouth open.

Thudding of her own heart. All the world shrinking around her, brought too close. The terrible sense of the two of them, only the two of them, in this room.

He doesn't look at her, only at the ceiling, rough and pitted, shadow and light, movement that never forms.

Say something, she finally says.

I'm sorry, he says, folding his arms and slumping, still not looking at her. I thought there'd be more.

He stares at his feet for another eternity. Stone floor unswept.

Well there will be more, she says. We'll have a wedding, there'll be a temple to Hekate, Pelias will have to give you the throne.

Yeah, he says.

You have to make these things true.

Jason says nothing.

The air hot and still. Medea feels as if she can't breathe. The ceiling so low, one chamber in a tunnel, only one exit.

Jason stands. I'm going to sleep.

He walks into the next room and she follows. There's a basin in the corner. He removes his sandals, cups water onto his feet, washing them. No drain, the water simply left on their floor. Sound of spattering against stone, flat and far away and disconnected.

The room big enough only for this basin and a bed. Almost no floor remaining. The bed rough pallets covered in linen, musty smelling. The linen feels damp to her hand.

Jason takes off the mantle, finishes undressing, washes himself slowly, methodically, as if in sleep already. Faced away from her, toward the corner.

When he's finished, he holds up the small cup for her. Snuff out the torch when you're done, he says, and he walks to the bed, three steps away, and lies down wet.

She stands there with the cup in this bare room and can't believe this is her life. But what can she do? It doesn't make sense to do anything except undress and wash herself. The water cold, a relief in this hot air. Washing with only her hand. No different than living in a cave. Her bare body in torchlight, the rest of the world gone. Even her skin seems not to be hers, looks foreign, dirty and dark from the sun, sore spots everywhere from sleeping on rope and rocks, and much thinner, bones close to the surface. This is all she has now.

She lies down beside him and feels the water evaporating from her skin, sucked by dry air. Mosquitos biting. Smaller things crawling in the bedding. She never thought she'd think of the Argo as a better place, but she does now.

She turns on her side, puts an arm over Jason's chest. More comfortable, at least, than lying on wood, and closer to him.

Rise and fall of his breath, the heat of him, and she's able to calm. The air closed in, but she tries not to think about it, tries not to think about their cave. Jason sleeps like a stone, a kind of anchor.

In the morning, he's gone, and the day is filled with attendants, preparations for a great feast. She's bathed and then waits, dressed and then waits, her hair arranged and then waits. So many hands touching her, something she hasn't experienced since Colchis. The indifference of slaves.

Touching her but absent, gone somewhere else, leaving her always alone, even when surrounded. She doesn't see Jason again until evening.

Wearing that red-and-purple mantle, despite the heat, and carrying the golden fleece. The two of them walk together to a large terrace. Iolcans gathered on all sides below, watching. Hundreds of Jason's people, and he looks like them. Same wide cheeks. Sent away as a baby, returned once before, now returned again. Pelias wanted him dead. Medea doesn't see any love for Jason. These people mute, only watching.

Jason turns his back to them, takes Medea's hand and they walk up enormous stone stairs. His hand shaking. White stone expanse, radiating heat. Only the two of them making this crossing.

Columns at the top of the stairs, a portico on another large terrace, and they walk through, spearmen lining either side. Pelias could have them killed easily.

At the far end of the portico, entrance to the throne room, massive stones that could not have been moved by men. As they enter, an enormous hearth at the center, raised, surrounded by four pillars that hold up the ceiling. Open center to this ceiling, for smoke and light. Pelias seated along a wall in plain view, surrounded by frescoes on the wall and floor, so that he is a dozen kings at once, with shield and spear, killing enemies, hunting, visited by goddesses. Golden king, shimmering on every side. Jason's fleece pale and shabby by comparison.

Pelias beckons, and they walk closer. Jason holds the fleece before him, a kind of shield as he approaches his uncle.

Bearded king, like all kings, face hidden, no longer a man but something else, closer to a god, mostly unseen. Holding a great spear of ash and bronze wrapped in gold. An attendant beside him holding the golden helmet and shield. This could be her father.

Medea wants to kill. She could take his spear and drive it through him. But she'd be dead before she could watch him die. Guards on all sides, ready. She'll have to wait for another time.

You are Medea, he says.

Yes.

You have killed your own brother, cut him into pieces, betrayed your father the king.

Yes.

Pelias smiles. And Jason. You have brought me something?

Jason holds out the golden fleece, dark sheepskin in this dim light.

Am I to believe that is the golden fleece?

It is, taken from Aeetes.

And how were you able to take it?

Jason looks at Medea. I had to yoke a pair of fire-breathing bulls.

Oh, Pelias says.

And sow the teeth of a serpent, teeth that grew into an army of earthborn men.

Pelias laughs. How did that army not kill you?

Jason looks again at Medea. I bathed in the river and dug a pit, away from all others. I sacrificed a ewe on a pyre and poured honey to Hekate, and when I walked away I didn't turn back, even when I heard the hellhounds.

Sensible, Pelias says.

At dawn, I steeped a charm from Medea in water, and anointed my body and my weapons.

And no spear from the earthborn men was able to pierce you?

I cast a stone in their midst when they rose up. They fought over that stone, slaying each other.

How did you know to do that?

Medea told me.

Well, Medea has been useful.

Yes, Jason says.

And what about the dragon guarding the golden fleece?

Medea put it to sleep.

Pelias laughs and keeps laughing, loud in this chamber.

Well, he finally says. We should have taken the fleece long ago. Great Aeetes apparently was willing to give it to anyone.

I betrayed my father for this fleece, Medea says.

Yes, I know. And butchered your brother. You've been very useful. If only you could have been here to prevent our tragedies.

What tragedies are those? Jason asks.

You were gone so long we thought the Argo was lost. We thought you had sunk, and your father Aeson was so distraught he drank poison.

Spear points of the guards already at Jason's chest, holding him back.

My brother was weak, Pelias says. Always weak. He was buried somewhere below, where there is no light, and fed very little, and his wife gone and one of his sons gone, but still if he wanted to be king, he should have acted like a king.

What about my brother Promachus? Where is he?

Your little brother drank poison too. I didn't see it, but that's what I'm told.

I'll kill you.

That's what I've been warned. One sandal. Flimsy for a prophecy, but there it is. Pelias sits forward on the edge of his throne, leans closer to Jason. They told me you were still-born. Did you know that? Your mother had women gather all around and weep because you were dead at birth. And it turns out this is true. You were stillborn.

Where is my mother?

Fucking some centaur, last I heard. Chiron, who raised you. If I believed in centaurs, though, I'd be in trouble, wouldn't I? I might even believe a sheepskin could have some strange power. So what was it like to be raised by a centaur? Do you run differently?

Jason's head low.

I'd like to see you run, to see whether you leap like a horse, to see whether you have hooves.

Pelias' men press forward with their spears, make Jason back away.

Run, Pelias says.

The spear points draw blood, Jason forced to turn and flee. More guards coming from the walls, penning him in, and these two spears advancing from behind. He can do nothing but run in a circle around the great hearth, young fabled king in the days before he is king, mantle flying out behind him, driven on by a wicked uncle. A story that won't be told, the humiliation. The soldiers behind are clever, their spear points coming in under the mantle and making small cuts on his back until Jason is in full flight.

Leap, Pelias yells. Jason does seem to leap whenever a spear cuts. Pelias laughing. Use your hooves, Jason. Your mother is getting away. There's still time. You could still have her, just like everyone else, every man and beast.

Jason no different from an animal, eyes wild, trapped, lungs and legs failing.

Stop, Medea shouts.

A great howl of laughter from Pelias. Stop she says. Okay. We'll stop for Medea. Because she has commanded.

His men return to their places, and Jason collapses to the floor panting.

Medea raises her arms, rolls her eyes back, chants to Hekate.

Ah, Hekate. You think I'm worried about Hekate? I'm the son of Poseidon.

She hears him walk closer and feels the slap, hard, that knocks her to the side.

I am the daughter of Aeetes, she says. Granddaughter of Helios and priestess of Hekate.

You are a whore and a slave. He gestures for his men. They come take her by the arms, pick her up kicking and twisting. Another man then at each leg and she's held aloft, limbs spread, helpless.

Hekate will rot you from the inside. Your guts will boil and come out your mouth in your own blood.

Vicious, Pelias says. But look at you now. I can do anything I like. Because I am king. You don't seem to understand the power of a king. I can rape you and make my men stand in exactly that position all night, still holding you there, and come rape you again in the morning. I can do this until you die. You can scream, and everyone in Iolcus can hear, and still I can do whatever I want. I can cut small pieces away from you and feed them to my soldiers and people while you watch. I can make them eat, and I can make you watch. I can say Poseidon demands it. I am his son, son of the sea god.

Medea would laugh, remind him that all kings claim this, remind him of the long generations that have come before, but she can see Pelias believes. Not in gods, not in Poseidon, but in power. He believes absolutely that his power is without limit, and he is capable of anything. His face close to hers now, hoping, ready and wanting to invent some new cruelty, something to eclipse all he has done before, and he would use her body for this.

I'm sorry, she says quietly. I understand now.

Pelias at the feast. Drinking wine, welcoming the Argonauts, shouting inanities, ripping at pieces of meat. Jason and Medea mute to one side, and just behind them, dozens of guards in the throne room, holding shields and spears, ready. This large terrace, columns and a view out to the sea. Long tables, guests and slaves.

The chair he sits in carved of oak, high backed, broad and raised. King above these other kings. Gray-black hair, pitted face dark, hidden by his beard. Rough large hands in fists, voice louder than any other. Wearing the skin of a lion, brought from some other land. Golden helmet set on the table before him, gold-wound spear at his side.

The fleece on the table, also, waiting, and finally Pelias stands. All Iolcans instantly quiet. Argonauts still shouting and laughing, but then they turn and see him and are quiet too.

Argonauts, he says. My guests. Welcome. Feast and drink and have whatever you want. You have brought my nephew back safely, and I will never forget that.

Pelias looks at the Argonauts, remains silent, lets each of them remember the prophecy and consider what they've done in returning Jason here.

He raises his hand and guards pour from the throne room, line up in ranks behind him, an even larger contingent arising from the broad stone staircase at the end of the terrace. They surround the guests on all sides, spear and shield and war helmet, then all is quiet again.

Pelias walks slowly around the table where he sits with Jason and Medea, his daughters and other family and court, stands in front and picks up the fleece in one hand, holds it high.

This is the skin of a sheep, he says. A simple skin. It has a bit of gold dust on it, gold which is easily removed or easily added. He scratches with a finger at the hide then holds up that finger to show the gold. Dust, he says.

He brings the fleece to the first table of guests, hands it to them. Each of you, hold this fleece, scratch off a bit of gold.

Pelias returns to stand before Jason, points at him. My nephew claims he has returned with the golden fleece, just as his father Aeson before him tried to claim my throne. Jason would have it now.

He lets his arm drop to his side. Argonauts, he says. Kings in your own lands. Do any of you have brothers or nephews?

He walks out among the tables. Would you like me to come to your home and stand at the side of your nephew as he asks for your throne? As he hands over a sheepskin sprinkled with a bit of gold dust and tries to call himself king?

Pelias raises both arms in the air, and his guards step closer on all sides, their spears lowered. The Argonauts remain seated. They are without shield or spear or helmet. They've already feasted and had too much wine. Pigs brought to slaughter.

A spear through each of you now. It would be easy. Or I can wait. Your lands are not far away. I can sail there on the Argo with my men whenever I hear of this nephew or brother or even some commoner who would challenge you. No son of a god but only a goatherd or a potter who would be king, and I can help him take your throne. Why can't any common fuck be king?

Pelias waves his arm and his men step away, spears upright.

Jason had a common birth. Aeson, his father, also had a common birth. We share a mother. But my father is Poseidon, weather god of the sea, ancient god. A god who shaped the world. And he shapes it still. He wants there to be a king. So he fucked my mother and made me to be king. Not Aeson, my common half brother, who has since proved his birth and his lack even of a will to live, by drinking poison along with another of his weak sons. And not Jason, who tries to trick his way onto my throne.

Pelias points to the sea. If I am killed, waves will form so great that each of your cities and peoples will be torn away, destroyed, vanished as if you had never been. That is my birthright. The return of the great flood if I'm slain. The anger of Poseidon come again. You don't want to anger my father, and you don't want to anger me.

He walks back around the table to his throne. Argonauts, he says. You see the sun beside us, over the far hills, low. You have until it sets. Get in your small fishing boats and go back to your huts. If you're still here when the sun touches, you're dead.

Pelias sits and takes a drink of wine, returns to eating. Some momentary disbelief in his guests, but then they rise and, seeing the sun low, begin to run. Great warriors in full flight, demigod kings not looking back, unsteady from the drink. Only the fisherman gives a backward glance at Medea. Then all are vanished down the steps.

Iolcans all waiting, no one moving. Only Pelias eats. Slow fall of the sun, sound of his chewing close beside Medea. She doesn't dare look at him.

Fishing boats appearing in the bay, small at this distance, rowing quickly in shadow, unable to know when the sun will touch, fanning out over the waters, scattering to many lands. Rushing to tell the tale of how they fled from Pelias after running his errands.

The sun darkening, wavering as it falls, and all are watching when it first touches. Pelias raises his arm and his guards at the stairs fall away from sight.

Acastus, Pelias says, loud for all to hear. My son. He places his hand on the shoulder of his son sitting beside him, young Argonaut, the only of the Argonauts remaining. Medea hadn't noticed him during the voyage, hadn't known he was the son of Pelias. Thin face, dark but not pitted like his father's. Tell us all, did the Argonauts intend to help Jason take my throne? Yes.

And is this fleece the golden fleece?

No.

Iolcans, Pelias says. Jason and Medea came here to deceive and destroy. They would make us all slaves. They brought an army from every land around. So what do we do with them now?

He waits, but of course no one speaks.

Acastus will be your king one day, when I am gone. Perhaps we should ask him.

Acastus stands, thin youth unlike a king, quiet in every gesture as if to compensate for his father. Medea is a priestess, he says, in his faint voice. Priestess of Hekate and of the Egyptian goddess Nute. She can fly and travel beneath the sea. Her voice can come from any direction, and she can see into another world and bend this world that we know. She is aided by a scorpion and by some other creature I cannot name, something from deep in the earth. She can also bring wind, and raise the seas. So we should cut out her tongue and her eyes and chop off her feet and hands and keep her in a room of stone, away from the ground and without any windows, unable to touch the wind or the sea or the night. We have to be careful not to touch her blood. I think she is something left over from an earlier time.

Pelias laughs. Sit, Acastus, sit. Only a boy. Medea is nothing. Pelias rises and grabs Medea by the hair, pulls her up and yanks her head back. Call on Hekate now, Medea. Call on her, bring your hellhounds, bend the world, raise the seas. Do something.

Her hair being ripped from her scalp, slow tearing, head yanked so far back she can't speak. She tries only to breathe.

No, we will not cut out her tongue and eyes and lock her away as something to be feared. She is nothing, and so she will be a slave. A simple house slave to my daughters and nothing more, and we will forget her.

Pelias lets go, and Medea is faint from the pain and lack of breath. Jason reaches for her, helps her to sit.

Jason will be a slave too, forgotten along with his father and brother and mother. I already can't remember them clearly. Did his father drink bull's blood or some other poison? Did Promachus drink also, or did I simply bash his head against the stone floor over and over? I can't remember. Did his mother flee to Chiron, or did she hang herself? These people are so small it's just impossible to remember what happened to them.

Pelias' daughters smiling. Several Medea's age, several much younger, still children. Shy in their viciousness but Medea is sure they will be like their father. Jason, if he were stronger, might rise now and claim his throne, rightful heir. He might demand vengeance for the murder of his father and brother, for the murder or banishment of his mother. He might make all Iolcans rise up against a tyrant with no legitimate claim to power. But the people of Iolcus do seem beaten and pliant, and what Pelias has said about the fleece is true for all to see, and the Argonauts are gone, scattered in fear. Medea does see that if Jason tried now he would only be killed.

She feels a need to protect him, strange feeling. As if she were his mother. He looks young and lost and without hope.

Take that ridiculous mantle off him, Pelias says, and dress them both as slaves. Take them now.

Guards unbuckle the purple-edged mantle and let it fall to the ground with all its unintelligible tales, pull Jason and Medea away along the edge of the terrace toward those stone stairs, Iolcans watching. Some of them smiling. Medea may have to destroy them all, not only their tyrant king.

Hovel of mud and sticks, rounded, just large enough to lie down, some human imitation of a hole or den, shelter from sun and night and nothing more. Pine straw for a bed. Rough clothing woven of goat hair, smelling of smoke and sweat and urine.

They spend the night stunned, without speaking, lying side by side, Jason's feet and head reaching the walls. Medea staring into a future transformed entirely. Her mind won't extend. It keeps stopping, can't imagine beyond these walls, can't imagine beyond this night. Tomorrow something that can't be reached or prefigured or believed. Medea destroyer of kings. Where is Medea now? Jason closer than ever before and still unknown.

No sky, no stars except through one small hole for smoke, for some fire imagined that can never happen. No room to sit beside it, and the entire hut would ignite. This land burning anyway, exposed, the sun close and no shade, all trees stripped away. A hundred similar huts on all sides of them, connected by dirt and shit.

The earth beneath her solid, unmoving, air close and heavy, everything slowing, a kind of burial. And how many years to be buried alive before being buried below? How many days? Time most frightening of all.

In the morning they are kicked awake and dragged by guards into the stone street before the citadel. Hot sun, hot stone. Pelias descending the wide steps from his terrace above, wearing the hide of a bull, two attendants behind carrying the great horns, yellowed bone heavy and smooth and curled and cruel even beyond death.

Pelias never known, always changing shape, born and reborn from somewhere beyond those massive stones. Spearmen always on every side, all alike and hidden behind helmets, become something other than human.

A crowd gathered, everyone pressing closer to see, and Jason and Medea at the center, held in place.

Iolcans, Pelias says, raising one arm. Jason and Medea would like to be married, so I have come to join them. Slaves who may not be parted.

His men bring heavy wet rope from the Argo, and Medea is pressed close against Jason, embracing him as the rope is wound from their calves upward, pulled tight with each turn, digging in. The two of them crushed against each other barely able to breathe.

The last tie cinched around her head, pressing her face into his neck. Some pose of affection enforced. Medea sucking a bit of air from the side of her mouth.

Pelias' men step away, she and Jason left to stand on their own in the sun.

I have welcomed my nephew home, Pelias says, and his young wife. I wish them every happiness.

Sandals on stone as he leaves with all his men, and the sounds of the crowd around them, the sun hotter and hotter, without mercy. Sweat from Jason's neck running into her eyes, stinging. She can't see or breathe.

The two of them a great weight up high being pulled off center, their legs farther and farther away below, shrinking, a base diminishing. Moments of laughter from the crowd, but most have left before long, only the stones remaining, a hundred smaller suns to match her grandfather above, able finally to punish, hanging directly overhead and pulling back the reins, holding in place, letting all burn.

All the same man: Helios, Aeetes, Pelias. Relentless, unforgiving, erasing all else, and this erasure must be fought. Medea will not fall. She wills herself and Jason upright, swinging above these burning stones, hands and arms and feet going numb, losing circulation. The ropes, tied wet, cinch tighter now as they dry. Practiced cruelty, torture. Her body and Jason's ground together, bone against bone. Creaking of lines around them, moored to the empty air. Feet becoming stumps, tiny spikes of feeling in otherwise dead slabs.

Jason's ribs sharpened. Knees become spears. Embrace of death, all set on fire until the world is without orientation. There is no sky, no ground, only burning. They are set free for a moment, weightless, the pain gone from her feet, then they hit stone so hard any last breath collapses. She has gone quiet inside, trying to recede and feel nothing, and she imagines the head of Promachus, Jason's young brother, smashed against these same stones over and over by Pelias, cannot understand the utter disregard for flesh. Only men can do this. Only men can treat flesh as nothing. And only men could have invented the idea of a king. Iolcans around them, but no one helps, held back by one man given the power of a god. All that would make them human given over and forgotten, no limit to what they will allow. Her arm searing against hot stone, no different from the meat of any goat or lamb. She and Jason have crossed over. They are no better than animals now.

Jason somehow is able to roll them sideways, her shoulder blade crushed. She feels the panic all through her, final struggle same as any animal or insect before annihilation, but then he rocks back harder the other way and she is lifted free. She rests on top of him, no longer against stone, no longer crushed or seared, and he has sacrificed. This is what breaks her, makes her weep though she can hardly breathe or move. Not the cruelty, but the kindness. Jason become real.

They are not cut free until the sun goes down. Knives tearing, and Medea wouldn't know if these were her limbs being severed. All numb and gone. She is barely conscious. No water. Drifting through the air. All day she has tried to remain awake so that Jason will not die. Some belief based on nothing, that if she doesn't sleep he will still be alive. At first she spoke to him, said his name, told him she loved him, told him not to die. Later she could only think these words, could no longer speak, but his chest still rose beneath her with every breath, slow and reassuring.

Impossible day, and impossible it could end. Separated, rolled onto stone still hot, looking upward into blue fading sky and closing her eyes again. Sound of Iolcans around them, many in the street, and someone props her up, pours water into her mouth. Shock of it, cool spread throughout her entire body. She opens her eyes to see Jason given water also, lies back down and sleeps.

When she wakes in darkness, no torch remains lit, only the moon. Stars washed out. The city turned to milk, stone smooth and cool and white. A world transformed, and no cruelty seems possible. All so still and soft. She's able to move her arms and legs, stiff and sore and weak but intact. She edges closer to Jason, puts her arm over his chest.

Jason, she says.

He has remained on his back, unmoved since morning, but she feels his hand on her arm. This won't last, he says. I promise.

Why did your father let your uncle do this?

He loved Pelias. And now everyone is gone. Father, mother, brother. I should have been here. The fleece was my idea. Pelias asked what I would do if I met the man who would destroy me. I said I would send him after the golden fleece.

So he believes you'll destroy him.

Yes.

Medea watches the moon, familiar and unknowable. All pattern clear and unseen. The story of Pelias and Jason. The story of Medea and anyone else: her brother Apsyrtus, Aeetes, Pelias, Jason, even Acastus. What shape, and when, all of us walking into traps set by ourselves and unremembered.

You have to promise me one thing, Medea says.

Yes.

That whatever happens, we won't be turned against each other.

How could that ever happen? he asks.

Just promise. For a time when all has slipped and become strange, even then.

I promise.

First love, Medea says. Only love. Pelias would make our wedding monstrous, but he has only made a stronger wedding. We were bound and nearly killed.

Wife, Jason says.

Until death.

Until death, he says.

Jason returning each day in darkness. White ghost covered in the dust of stone, curls of his hair the color of milk, some creature born of night and silence and dimly shining, faint replica of her husband lying down to hold her in his arms and then gone. Minutes each day left to them and nothing more. His arm heavy, grown larger quarrying to build more monuments to Pelias. Welts everywhere from whips, on his back and arms and legs and chest. He will do this unnumbered days until his body is old and broken, then they will lay him inside a wall, let him become one of these stones.

Medea rising early with him, in darkness still. No daylight is theirs, all light given over. Slavery a walking sleep, and

Medea the lowest of the slaves. She is to serve the daughters of Pelias, but she will never see these daughters. She removes their shit and piss and blood, washes their clothing and pottery, sees every sign of their existence, every leaving, feels its texture in her fingers, smells each of them, knows their scent and health and moods, all without direct visitation, and so in her mind each of them takes on a shape and character, not unlike a god.

Alcestis of every scent from every land, cinnamon and musk and oils Medea cannot recognize, searching always for something behind these fainter and constant that could be called Alcestis, some breath or other trace, and Medea knows she discovered this already from the first moment but somehow can never remember it or give it shape. Polluted by every stronger scent in layer after layer. Suitors are being brought to her, endless suitors, and all that she has worn is enough for a hundred women, finest linen and smoother, lighter cloth Medea has never known, every pattern and color. Most is from Egypt. Without Egypt, every land would remain in barbarity. Every figure made in clay by an Iolcan or Mycenaean or Korinthian is Egyptian, every pattern drawn, the cut of each cloth, until Medea wonders whether there is anything at all that can be called Iolcan.

Alcestis most elusive of gods, not wanting a husband, able to wait centuries. Never able to say no but never saying yes. Becoming nothing, and so every man must want her. She will never contradict any idea of her. She is without limit. She has found some other world to dwell in and no longer feels the roughness of this one, and Medea must find this also. Each moment of slavery become nothing.

Medea is beaten every few days, whether she does her work or not. At first, she worked harder, or refused to work, but now she understands why she is beaten, because the hand holding the stick or the leather strap is also the hand of a slave. Pleasure and self-hate and a refusal impossible marked by each sting, recorded.

What she returns to is scent, buries herself in what has been soiled and discarded, thrilled most by Amphinome and Evadne. Old enough almost for suitors, waiting their turn, impatient, tearing at garments, spilling and breaking.

The younger daughters impossible to separate. Peisidike, Pelopia, Hippothoe, Antinoe, Antiope, Asteropeia. Grimy play, reckless, dirt and leaves without perfumes or oils, but at least two of them are almost the age of Amphinome and Evadne, larger clothing, the beginning of scent, and Medea doesn't know who these two might be. No one will speak with her. Outcast among slaves, priestess of darkness feared and hated and beaten, foreign barbarian.

Some agreement among slaves and guards, everyone waiting for her to break and then what? What do they believe will be revealed? What do they think she could possibly be hiding? Nute and Hekate far away. Jason knows there is no scorpion in his chest. She has lost all power.

Her only reprieve the sea. Washing clothing at the shore, left alone, burning sun but when it falls beyond the hill all is softened. Gentle surge of waves over her feet. White rock cooled by wet cloth, darker rock below, sea urchins in every hollow. Fish banded yellow and blue, smaller fish like white mottled toads, pairs of eyes and all else camouflaged. Hiding, same as Medea.

She is called from her washing one evening, hurried up to the citadel. Brought to a bedroom large and lavish, walls painted like pottery, thin black figures everywhere against white. Woven cloth hanging, stone arranged in pattern on the floor. Two of Pelias' daughters waiting with whips in their hands, and Medea is left alone with them.

You are Medea, the older one says.

Yes.

I am Evadne.

I know you, Medea says. Hating your sister Alcestis, waiting for her to leave, wanting a man. So desperate you would take any man. I can smell the stink of it in everything you wear.

Evadne fat from sloth, hair oiled black. Lie down on the floor. On your back. No clothing.

Medea strips, watching the other sister, years younger, still a child. What is your name? she asks.

Asteropeia.

Beautiful Asteropeia, Medea says. You fear Evadne, and you should fear her.

Now, slave, Evadne says.

Medea walks to the center of the room and lies down.

Hands over your head, Evadne says, and now Medea is exposed, lying naked on stone, stretched out, her belly and breasts bare.

Evadne steps close, caresses Medea with the end of the leather strap, the lightest touch, watching the leather brush over skin.

I will tell you a secret, Medea says. You will be the only ones to know. Not even Jason knows.

Evadne's hand stops, the strap resting against Medea's belly. Tell.

I am pregnant, Medea says.

You lie.

I am the priestess of Hekate and Nute. Nute who swallows the sun each night and gives birth to each day. Ancient god, Egyptian god. Hekate who rules all that lives in the night. And if you kill this child, you will never have your own child. One month when you bleed, the blood will not stop until you die.

Evadne's arm quick as a snake, the whip invisible, sudden pain across Medea's bare breasts. Medea curls and howls and sucks at the air. Pain like flame, pulse and rise and heat discovered from nothing, unbearable and then stronger still.

Call on Hekate now, Evadne says. You are no priestess.

Medea can't speak.

Lie on your back. Arms over your head.

Medea tries to stretch out again, closes her eyes, hears the leather through air and feels the whip again across her breasts. She curls and her lungs heave, as if she is sobbing, but no sound.

Barbarian, Evadne says. Acastus was right. You are from another time, something left over. Some beast. And we should cut off your feet and hands and cut out your tongue and eyes. Not because you might call on any god, but because you are an animal. Stretch out again.

Medea can't make herself do this, but Evadne pulls one of her arms, kicks her in the back, and this is a new pain, dull and deep. Asteropeia, Medea gasps. Please.

Asteropeia won't help you. She will do what I say.

Evadne stretches Medea and pins her arms against the stone. Her face close, looking down into Medea's eyes, heavy hot breath, enjoying this. Whip her, she says.

Asteropeia only a girl, not yet fully grown, a child caught in something that can't be understood. Holding a strap of leather and walking closer very slowly until she stands at Medea's side. Innocent and frightened.

Now, Evadne says. Whip as hard as you can.

But Asteropeia is frozen, staring into Medea's gray eyes, wolf's eyes. She believes. She believes everything about Medea.

Hekate, Medea calls, chants in their tongue, tear the womb from every daughter of Pelias. Even this innocent. Reach inside her with your bare wolf's claws and rend until no wall is smooth.

Cold forest, air the sound of water, track of fear. Medea must bring this forest close, make its breath visible. She stretches her jaw forward, teeth bared, feels her spine hunch and screeches from all that is terror. She twists and bites Evadne's arm, clamps and locks her jaw.

Medea dragged over the floor by her mouth as Evadne tries to escape. Atavistic pleasure, sinking teeth into flesh, sucking air from the corners of her mouth, shaking from her neck trying to rip flesh from bone. Deepest pleasure.

Evadne in full flight now, some ape struggling low over the floor, bent on hand and foot, made a beast herself, rumored horror from far beyond Egypt, screaming. Whip forgotten. Slave forgotten. No daughter of a king but only an animal maimed. Dragging her arm with this demon attached. When she rips free, Medea tastes blood, rolls onto all fours, corners

Asteropeia. Hackles raised, teeth clicking. The girl alone now with the beast.

Loose forest floor, all that has fallen and decayed. Mist in the trees, their tops gone, known only by wind, rising along every ridge. Quiet place of listening and waiting, sound impossible to locate, lost in mountains, lost in cold.

Asteropeia pressed into a corner, still holding the leather strap. Dark frightened eyes, pulse visible in her neck, beating fast.

Medea could devour. Some deep need to kill and tear and taste more blood, and her prey frozen, unable to move, unable to make a sound. Closer and the pull at her spine twisting her sideways, unbearable, lifting her into the air, a thrill that would make her lunge. Flat stink of fear. She opens her jaws and wants this child, aches and hears a moan from inside her, low and desolate and strange.

Medea returns to her washing at the shore, watches the half-moon rise, heavy and rounded. She can almost see the dark half of it, some sense of that hidden orb, its felt outline against darker sky. White rock around her mirroring. Second sun, night sun, the form Medea would take, granddaughter of Helios worshipping night. Drawn without chariot, some liquid movement within Nute, within skies contained.

Form inside her just as impossible, just as difficult to reach or believe. Some other moon, night-body, following its own movement. Medea slaps wet clothing against rock, swings and breathes and small waves break around her, but she's listening, also, for something else, same as trying to hear the slow glide of the moon, some hollow lost within other sound.

When she's finished with her work, she slips into the water, cool and clean, salty and dark, and swims out far beyond the shore into the deep. Surface opaque from the moon, no stars below and only faint above, held in this barrier between worlds. Medea now and Medea with child. Dangling at the roof of the world unknown, all that will be.

Born into slavery. Pelias able to reach her child at any moment to bash a soft head on stone. Jason gone.

Nute, Medea says to the night. Hekate. If this child is better dead, then take it now. Don't let Pelias take it.

Medea spreads her legs beneath the waves. Take it now if it will be no more than a slave.

BOOK TWO

Cauldron of bronze large enough to hold a body. How it was forged, Medea cannot imagine. Tin and copper melted, enough to form a pool, and from that pool rose some hand that could paint liquid onto air, shape walls burning and hold them in place until all cooled. Story of how what was once shapeless hardened and why we've taken these forms and not others.

Surface pitted and stained and worn, figures hidden, encased, soundless, revealed by fire and vanished again. Years of standing before this one cauldron, before this fire, punishment from Evadne. Boiling day and night, wellings in liquid never the same twice, watching source and revelation.

Asteropeia visits nearly every night. A young woman now, no longer a child, she imagines Medea knows every dark way, and Medea lets her imagine this. Medea a mother to her and also ready to kill her, for years now.

Medea's own children without a mother, two sons left each day to scratch at the dirt and wait, slaves too young yet to be of use, fattened for a future they can't possibly believe.

Asteropeia's face wet from the heat, beading, hair soaked, and so beautiful. She does not want a suitor. She wants Hekate.

Find something I can give to my father, she tells Medea. Something that will be enough. Something to release me.

Night after night of this, Medea silent, staring into broth and stew, watching scum on the surface for signs. Waiting for chunks of meat tumbling in darkness and brought to the surface to breach and leer and be devoured again. Her sons will be old enough soon, so she must find something.

She would look also to the stars, but Evadne has placed Medea's cauldron in a small stone room with a low ceiling and one tiny window. Wood for fuel stacked along the walls, goats and sheep led in bawling, crowding into the corners, trying to escape flame. Medea made butcher and fire keeper and cook. For her, the rest of the world has nearly ceased to exist. A few hours in the final darkness of each night to sleep, to hold Jason and her sons and try to remember, then she returns for all the long day and most of the night and forgets again.

Asteropeia's skin so soft even wet, faint down of her neck and even her eyebrows Medea would like to lick. Her mouth opens whenever Asteropeia comes near, and she wants to devour. Young skin, no line or crease or slack, lit by some other heat, a fullness to it.

Condemned to burning, this room of fire radiating back from every wall, so Medea no longer wears clothing, only her own sweat, and Asteropeia, too, stands naked beside her, shadowed curves and fire skin flickering, shapes across her belly and breasts and neck. Medea watches here too, uses her hand to trace image, and Asteropeia stands without moving, closes her eyes and memorizes.

Forms of what will be, Medea says. Shape in shadow, in pulse. Asteropeia listens. Medea's hand sliding down to hold a breast with stretched hand, pulling downward as if this bulb could be planted.

Youth, Medea says. All you have to offer is youth.

Asteropeia's lips parted, eyes closed, swaying where she stands. Medea's hand grasping impossible flesh. Your father can be made young. We can rejuvenate him. That's the gift that will set you free.

Asteropeia's eyes open. You can do that?

Bring another of your sisters, and bring an old ram. Tomorrow night. We must hurry, before the moon changes. I will make this ram young, and then we'll do the same for your father.

Joy pure and simple in Asteropeia, clinging to Medea now, soft breast against breast, and Medea's mouth on her neck, breathing in desire, unbearable.

Later she walks alone down to the sea, immerses as she does every night, to cool and wash off the sweat and smell and all of her existence. She holds her breath, sinks below the surface, holds her arms around her breasts as if she were holding Asteropeia, slow fall into darkness, lost and without sound.

More and more difficult each night to surface, to leave water and walk up the hill to her home, round mud hovel not much larger than her cauldron. She pushes in between Jason and her sons, smells their filth, dense hot cloud as stifling as the room of fire and vapor, scent of rock and feel of Jason turning to stone, skin become dust and flesh hardening beneath, returning to the first form of earth god, ledge and weight compacting layer upon layer until his footsteps will sink.

She lies on her side, turned away from Jason, and wraps an arm around her sons. Thin, unlike children, smelling like goats, smelling of shit caked on their hands and feet and knees, flinching in their sleep and grabbing at shapes in the air. When they wake, they will talk without pause, questions and telling her everything about nothing. She doesn't know if this is their age or because they have only a few waking moments together. Medea has never spent a full day with her children. She doesn't know what they should be or who she should be. All she can do is put her arm around them, breathe in their acrid scent, and sleep.

Old ram, brains gone and replaced by bone, huge shelf of a head above dark senseless eyes, caverns of time and silence and no recognition. Refusing to be pulled in any direction, crabbing sideways then butting hard against a leg. Dark white in the moon, full curl of horns rough and patterned, unfelt scars and forgotten battle.

Medea and Asteropeia and one of her sisters all struggling in the yard, trying to reach the door. Bleating of sheep and goats from within, roar and heat of fire, smell of meat and blood boiling, and the ram somehow knows. Black mouth biting, then lowering his head again, hooves opening furrows in the hard ground.

Three ropes around him now: around his horns, cinched high around a front leg, and catching a hind hoof. They pull him backward, hind leg first, make him hop. Medea without mercy, feeling nothing, yanking her way back into the room. This ram could be Pelias and she would pull the same.

Every sheep and goat inside smelling the old ram, bleating and pushing away from him into corners, knocking over piles of wood, legs caught and tumbling, chaos. At the threshold, he butts hard enough to raise dust from the wall. Leaping now and falling hard as his legs are pulled out, scrabbling up, hooves against stone, head and neck bucking at the air. A form of king, unable to believe, dominion absolute.

Asteropeia standing close, fearless, pulling at the rope around his horns. True believer, without hesitation. Her sister backing farther away but still holding her rope, an accomplice suitable enough, thick and strong.

Medea reaches for an ax, dark blade of bronze, newly sharpened, hands it to Asteropeia, who is yanked hard now by only one arm. The ram still charging, wanting the open night.

Now, Medea yells. Kill the ram. Chop off his head.

Asteropeia drops the rope, raises the ax in both hands. Beautiful even in slaughter, swing of her young breasts, mouth open and insane and perfect, warrior more terrible than any demigod king. When this is her father, the blade will come down just as certainly. In his bed in some mammoth chamber of stone and hide, his two daughters let in without question, in darkness as he sleeps. All Medea can hope for is that the first blow doesn't kill, that he is only maimed, a shoulder hanging, and tries to rise up, sees his beautiful daughter swinging the ax again, innocent Asteropeia, believing she's making her father young.

The ram shakes his head, free now, sees night, dull blackness to mirror the void inside, and rears back for his final charge, but the blade slices thick muscle at his neck, breaks open his spine, and all limbs fail, fall to the floor, hard stone. Eyes open, still alive, still willing movement impossible. Medea wants this moment for Pelias, only a few strings of flesh connecting, no response but still willing, still knowing. She wants him to know this was her doing.

Asteropeia, she says. You must say these words before his eyes are gone. Medea releases you of your old flesh. Hekate will make you young again.

Asteropeia holds the ax high and yells, Medea releases you of your old flesh. Hekate will make you young again. Then she swings again and severs the ropy neck.

Yes, Medea says. Yes. You must say this to your father before his eyes fade. He must know.

We can't do this, Asteropeia's sister says. Still holding the rope taut. Young and plump and blank as any beast, and Medea would slaughter her too. Medea made a slave, for years. She would slaughter every one of them now.

What's your name? Medea asks.

Peisidike.

Is Peisidike the daughter who wants her father to grow old and die? Does she want to be the one who denied his second youth? Watch what happens to this old ram, and then decide. It will be up to you. We will make your father young only if you say to do it.

No, Peisidike says. I can't be the one to decide.

You will decide.

Mask of fear, Peisidike lost. Still holding that rope, unable to move.

Cut him into thirteen pieces, Medea says. Quick, before his blood cools. He must be in the cauldron before he loses his last heat.

Asteropeia hacks at a shoulder. Peisidike, she yells to her sister. Pull the leg so I can sever the joint.

Medea smiles. Such a willing butcher.

Peisidike helps, finally, kneels to pull at each leg as Asteropeia hacks. Spray of filth over Peisidike's face with every chop, blood and small bits of flesh and bone. She's too stunned even to look away. She has no hope of resisting. She will pull at her father's leg as Asteropeia severs.

Dismembered, headless trunk, but there must be thirteen pieces, so Asteropeia hacks into ribs. Foam of lungs flung as she yanks the ax free, this room a cavern of gore and fire, wet sopping sound when she strikes again. Cauldron waiting.

Hurry, Medea yells. His blood must still be hot.

Medea puts an ax in Peisidike's hands, makes her chop at the spine to separate pelvis from ribs.

Upper cage opened by Asteropeia, and Medea tells her to reach in for the heart. Asteropeia to her elbow in blood and foam with a knife comes out with a slick muscle and holds it high. Ancient form, some scream from deep within her as she sees the heart bare.

Yes, Medea says. Throw that in the cauldron. First piece.

Asteropeia shaking from the thrill, head twisting, throwing this heart and returning to her ax to hack at spine.

Peisidike has severed the lower part and stands frozen again. Cut off his balls, Medea yells at her. Now.

So Peisidike kneels on the wet floor and folds the testicles and penis and hide over the sharp blade, slices until they're free.

Medea pulls her to her feet and brings her to the edge of the cauldron, hot dark bronze radiating. She whispers in Peisidike's ear. You will make your father young, she says. Only you. You are the one with the power to do this. You are a priestess. Hekate favors you.

Peisidike frightened but also stupid enough to believe. Soft flesh raised for nothing.

What makes him old is in his balls, Medea says. Old ram same as your father. His children have taken his life. But if you break each one in your teeth and then spit into the cauldron, all that constrains him will be broken. This is how he will be made young again. Death will lose its hold.

Peisidike looks at the dark meat in her hands, wet hide, testicles unsheathed and wrapped in vein or worse. But she raises this horror to her mouth, bites into a testicle, breaks it, and vomits onto the floor.

Only one more, Medea says. One more and you'll release him. Peisidike about to faint, pale even in firelight, eyes wet and mouth still gagging. But she bites into the other testicle, releasing some flood that opens her mouth in awful grimace.

Throw them in now, Medea says. And spit his seed, also, into the cauldron, to make him new.

Peisidike throws the bloody pelt into the cauldron and spits.

Help your sister now, Medea says.

Able butchers chopping the torso. Ropy entrails endless, slick iridescent orbs of organs sliced, thick overpowering smell of bile, of all that rots inside, and how are thirteen pieces to be counted?

So Medea tells them he's ready. All pieces into the cauldron, she says. They throw flesh and bone and hide into the dark stew that already contains other meat and blood and will contain more.

Medea with a long thin paddle made of wood stirs the great vat, pushes the pieces of the ram under, chants to Hekate in her barbarian tongue, song unintelligible to the sisters. Hekate, she calls. Tonight I kill a king. My sons will not be slaves. I will not be a slave. My husband will not be a slave. Tonight I kill a king and feed his balls to his daughter. Hacked into pieces with no burial, no funeral rites, fed to his family. Son of Poseidon cooked in a stew. The only great waves to form will be from whatever I stir. I will rule Iolcus, and all will be my slaves, and my sons will walk on streets of flesh.

Torches, Medea says to Asteropeia and Peisidike in their ugly tongue. Light torches in the fire and go outside to pray to the moon, to Hekate, for this old ram to be made young. We must pray to Hekate until a young lamb emerges from the cauldron. That body is forming now, but we must help it along, help Hekate and Nute give birth in night.

Asteropeia in a kind of trance, mute and doing whatever Medea says. Peisidike not as strong, at the edge of collapse, but this is only the beginning. She has work to do.

They light their torches in the fire beneath the cauldron and step outside as Medea stirs and stokes and chants. Old prayers to Hekate, from Colchis, from when she would sacrifice a lamb or a goat. Take these pieces, dismember all, separate night from day and let day never be found again. Let all but your priestess wander without light.

She was only a girl then, and she always imagined the form of a wolf, Hekate as wolf somewhere behind her in the trees, watching, ready to devour but waiting. When she'd return the next night, the carcass was always gone, dragged away, bones scattered.

She will wait long enough for Asteropeia and Peisidike to despair, to lose all faith and believe the old ram is gone. They must believe Medea and Hekate have failed. Staring into that moon, they should feel its distance, cold, unreachable, and hear their torches in the wind, a tearing of empty air, shield against nothing. They must feel alone.

Solid weight of head and horns deep in the cauldron. Medea pries with the paddle from the edge, lifts the old ram as she will lift the head of Pelias, just to let him fall again. Boiled in blood, sharing the stew with the ram. If any creature rises, it will be half man, half ram, entrails intertwined, half covered in hide, half bare, heads fused. Pelias' head mounted on the back of the ram's, teeth snapping at the sky. Brain turned to bone, without memory, arms half buried in the ram's back, hands useless on short stumps, legs gone below. Wandering trackless, never seeing what will come, staring without shelter into the bare sun. Even this would be too good for Pelias.

Clot of wool in one corner of the room, the sheep jammed in so thick, all their butts facing her, afraid to turn their heads to see what's coming. The goats much craftier, edging for the door. Medea grabs the youngest lamb, bleating, and flings it into the air above the cauldron.

Asteropeia! she yells. Peisidike!

The lamb hits with all four legs wide spread. Dark stew red brown and thick taking shapes in the air, as if some new phantom might form or be read, augury of all to come. Vanished too quickly, spattered against floor and walls and wasted, Medea not quick enough. White wool submerged, but she reaches in with her bare hand, burning, and pulls the lamb free as the sisters appear. Midwife to an unnatural birth, lamb pulled from welter and gore of a ram, no need of a womb. She drops it bleating onto the stone floor and douses it with fresh water from an urn to stop the burning.

Asteropeia falls to the floor, hugging the lamb, weeping, laughing, a madwoman. No butcher after all. Peisidike aghast at what powers might be. Medea pulls her close. Peisidike, she says. Hekate favors you. Will you give your father a new youth? Will you let him be reborn?

Yes, she says quietly, clearly without thought, only staring at the lamb, this concoction of air, impossibility made real. Brown burning thing emerged from darkness screaming new life.

The moon too bright, every stone in relief, the air itself illuminated and shortened. When she passes a guard, there is no distance. She walks slowly, careful not to run, takes her usual path to the sea to bathe and then home. She must hold her sons and Jason one last time. She knows she may not survive the night.

The sisters washed and naked, carrying their clothing in their hands, axes hidden within. No unusual thing for the many daughters of Pelias to visit him at night. Every girl and young woman in a kingdom belongs to the king, even his own daughters.

The guards let them in, and the sisters cross an open stone floor in darkness. They will let the garments fall. No guards in here. Only two daughters, naked, axes held high, stepping closer to their father.

Asteropeia's love for Medea, her trust, her innocence and pure belief. The pain of this makes Medea want to howl. But still, she would have every king in every land lie asleep tonight while his daughters step closer with axes.

Medea pulls her sons so close and tight they squirm away even in sleep, refusing. She has only moments left. Asteropeia and Peisidike will return to the cauldron not only with the body of their father but also with every one of his guards and with his son, Acastus. The sisters know to wrap the pieces of Pelias in cloth, but they didn't ask how no one would notice. Most likely Pelias will scream and the guards will come in before he's dead. Maimed and his beautiful daughter Asteropeia above him swinging her ax again, chopping deep into his flesh then telling him, Medea releases you.

Scent of her children, something buried deep within all other smell that hooks at her spine and lungs and can never be dislodged. She would protect them even as Jason is dragged away, even as she herself is torn to pieces. Animal and unknowable. She has put them at risk now in order to save them, to keep them from being slaves, but this risk is too terrible. She would go back and undo everything.

Nute, she calls inside without sound. Allow passage through this night. Let my sons remain whole.

She buries her nose in their necks, one last breath each to memorize, and then rises.

Moon almost full, bright world of shadow. Her bare feet on dirt and stone. She knows it may be Pelias waiting when she returns to the cauldron. Holding the axes she gave to his daughters, waiting with his men, ready to torture. That room of fire and stone, hot bronze of the cauldron, all that she might fear.

Iolcus quiet. Sound of her feet only, and perhaps nothing will happen, the sisters too afraid.

Her low room looks like a stone shepherd's hut from outside, uneven walls and roof, bare yard. But far too bright, glowing with heat, the only large flame on this hillside every night, burning through every small crack and hole in constellation, as if Helios could be contained.

Medea steps into this inferno for the last time. Whatever happens tonight, all will be broken. She will not come here again. Even if the sisters do nothing, she will take an ax and go to Pelias herself.

Thick ash beneath the cauldron, gray and lit by coals still red, patterned like snakes fallen jointed. Broom of sticks, and when she sweeps, the ash collapses and coals submerge. Buried and sinking farther still into some abscess yet undiscovered where even stone has been consumed.

She sweeps ash and coal toward the door, levels it, hidden and waiting. Anyone who comes for her will walk on coals first.

Then she rebuilds the fire, packs it tight, fans new flame. Let Helios rekindle here. Let this room be unbearable to all who enter, even the walls ignited. Sheep and goats tethered in the corners no longer bleating. Low terrified moans, succumbing to heat, collapsing. Medea douses herself in water, drinks and steams as if appearing suddenly from another world, naked and terrible and ready to destroy all.

She hears them outside, tramp of soldiers and women lamenting, the other daughters of Pelias no doubt, a great crowd on the run, the entire citadel, and smiles. The sisters have done their work.

Pelias enters first, headless. Borne by guards, body hacked and naked and misjointed, pulling apart, ribboned by axes. Blood turned dark already.

Soldiers crushing coals, one of them with feet bare and falling now with a scream against the cauldron, where he sticks momentarily then tears himself away. The cauldron itself unmoved, heavy center to the world, immutable, holding all. Pelias dropped onto ash and coal and stone, guards trying to lift again something too loose to be held, a body that can unfold infinitely.

Acastus at the door, thin boy, no king, holding his father's head high for her to see. Dipped in blood, hair wet and dark. Mouth loose, cave hole without sound. Eyes alive still, almost, large and whited and gazing somewhere beyond her. Head of her father, head of Helios, head of every king and king to be, but her brother's head was not the same. If she could go back, it would be her father's head this time.

Medea, Acastus says. His voice is fear, thin and swallowed.

Where are the waves? Medea asks. The great flood returned. The son of Poseidon slain. We should all run for higher ground.

My father, Acastus says. Bring him back to life.

Medea laughs. So that my slavery can be endless? Shall I make him immortal? Perhaps I can fuse a whip to each hand, or give him claws to tear at my back. Or the tail of a scorpion. Do you remember the scorpion?

Acastus squinting away from the fire, too bright and hot, his father's head no longer held high but sagged against his leg, heavy. His soldiers backing against the walls, body abandoned in ash.

Bring him to the sea, Medea tells him. Let Poseidon make him whole.

Acastus steps outside and returns with Asteropeia and Peisidike, each held by a guard. They are naked and spattered in blood. Medea would have all vanish and only Asteropeia remain. Sea nymph. If all women have been only one woman, if Medea's mother and grandmother were the same and descended from another woman also the same, the Titaness Tethys, then Asteropeia is the ideal form all would return to. Medea herself would take this form.

Daughters, Medea says. Daughters of a king. Peisidike is the one who made an old ram young, who bit into what made him old and let him come back as a lamb. I witnessed it here myself. She is favored by Hekate.

All eyes on Peisidike, who is too frightened to speak. Brought close to her father's mutilated form.

Let me go, Asteropeia yells. His blood must still be hot. Thirteen pieces. Tell them, Medea.

True believer, innocent, terrible to ruin. If only Medea had known Asteropeia in Colchis or anywhere else. Medea says nothing, and Asteropeia breaks free of her guard, grabs an ax and hacks at a shoulder. Dull slap of metal into meat and hollow sound of bone. Peisidike! she screams.

Her sister unable to move, only watching, so Asteropeia is alone. All Pelias' men pressed back against the walls. Acastus the runt-king afraid. Rising laments outside, some great crowd just beyond the door. Asteropeia swings her ax and brings it down each time with a low grunt, tearing through all that would age her father, releasing death's hold.

She opens his rib cage and falls to her knees to reach in through lung to tear out his heart. A knife, she yells. Bring me a knife.

Medea only watches, does nothing. No one helps Asteropeia. So she rises and takes her brother's knife and drops again onto what remains of her father, reaches in and is his blood still hot? Her fingers around slick muscle of his heart and the knife cuts all that would bind, frees it to the air. Our father will be made young again, she tells her brother as she throws new meat into the cauldron.

What is this, Medea? Acastus asks. What have you done?

Your sisters brought me an old ram and cut him into thirteen pieces. Peisidike bit into what had made him old, and I stirred as she and Asteropeia called to Hekate, outside with the moon. I saw a shape forming and called for them as a new lamb sprang from the cauldron, the old ram made young.

You have made my sisters butcher my father. You have bent the world again and distorted all.

Asteropeia wants to make her father young again, a gift, and she is led by Peisidike, who is favored by Hekate or some other dark god more powerful than I have known myself. Bringing a body back to life goes beyond what I can do. I have only stirred, as Evadne has had me do for years now. Everyone is witness that I have not killed the king. I have not brought him here or chopped at him with an ax or ripped out his heart.

Asteropeia cleaves a shoulder, white bone and joint with pale membrane that catches the light of flame, some new life in Pelias, reborn of fire, no son of Poseidon at all. Tended still by a sea nymph exiled to a grim world of blood and ash. She works alone, hacking and grunting in shadow light, flinging one arm into the cauldron and then the other.

Medea stirs, dark stew that will fuse old ram and old king. Let muscle and vein connect, she chants in her tongue. Let the head of Pelias live within the stomach of the ram, let him scream and scream and never be heard, encased in flesh.

Arc of the ax flung over and over, wet slap into thick hams, severing a leg, torso turned downward into whatever might lie below and be seen without eyes. One legged, armless, headless, basted in ash, and his daughter works to free him. Peisidike! she yells again.

Acastus, Medea says. Peisidike must do what she did before. Why won't she bring your father back to life?

Peisidike broken, held up by a guard, unable even to look toward the body, but her brother slaps her, grabs her arm and forces her to her knees. He shakes their father's face in hers. Bring him back, he roars. Some blood of Pelias in him after all.

Peisidike given an ax, and she turns her head as she chops.

Hurry! Asteropeia yells at her. His blood is going cold.

Limbless torso turned on its side, and the sisters hack through flesh until they reach spine. A popping sound. Peisidike can tear through the last ropes of entrails now, last thin strands of muscle connecting his hips and groin to his back. Awaking to her task. She kneels close to slip the blade of a knife under his balls. Shriveled and coated in blood and ash, hidden, but she rips them free as Asteropeia crushes through ribs and folds his back in two.

Segmented king, faceless and neutered, returning to some earlier form. Summoned by his daughters. Slack scrotum searched for its two eggs, Peisidike's tongue and teeth finding other wet flesh until she sucks in the first small orb and bites down, gagging, spitting into the cauldron.

Seed into the stew, Medea says in Colchian, barbarian. Fed to his daughters, and everyone will have a taste of this king, even the dogs. Demigod meat.

Scrotum a loose second chin for Peisidike as she searches with her tongue. Held in both hands, eyes closing, at the edge of the cauldron. Something Medea wishes Pelias could have seen. Peisidike grown from his seed and returning to the source. Plump young flesh wet in firelight, believing herself a priestess, favored, biting down a second time to crush what remains of kingdom, spitting and tossing this flap of skin to join the other parts.

Medea stirs.

Asteropeia is quartering the back. Two arms, two legs, head, heart, hams, groin, guts, and quartered back, ribs protruding. Thirteen pieces. The daughters heave together for the larger chunks, heavy plunge into the stew, spilling over the sides to hiss in the fire. A few remains must be searched for in the ash, the last of the entrails, daughters on their hands and knees, and then they are ready.

Throw in his head, Asteropeia yells. Quickly.

Acastus hesitates. He warned his father about Medea. He would have kept her from the earth and air and fire and blood and sea, all that she might travel through or summon, and he must wonder now where she might take his father once he gives over the head. Medea smiles. Acastus will be next in the stew, and then his sisters, all but Asteropeia. All who were close to Pelias, all but her, will be going into the pot.

Our father must emerge whole, Acastus tells Medea. Young and in one piece.

Peisidike is the favored one. She is the one who brought the old ram back.

Do not make a monster. You have sons, Medea.

I will do nothing for your father unless you agree that I am no longer a slave, and my sons, and Jason. We are all free now or you can stir this mess yourself and invoke whatever god you please. But I am only helping Peisidike. She is the one who must make your father young. She came from his seed and has released his seed.

Acastus raises his father's head, looks on that terrible face one last time, and flings him into the cauldron. You have your freedom, he says. Make my father whole.

Hekate, Medea chants in barbarian tongue. Hekate, first among gods, let all remain separate, let no pieces join unless his shattered balls become his eyes and he wears his skeleton on the outside, encased in bone. No legs and no arms. Let his throat be lined with the old ram's hide, and his mouth be the ram's anus. Let him hear only his inner workings, ears buried deep inside. And let him live a thousand years, slowly growing, filling with blood. Let him make new blood and never release it.

The daughters of Pelias worship Hekate and the moon, hold their firebrands to the sky. All people of Iolcus on their knees before that bright falling orb, begging the god of Medea. Terrible waste of years, but all is coming to pass.

In her room alone with fire and steam, stirring the pieces of Pelias and the ram, making stew and nothing more, old meat cooking through. Poseidon quiet. All the world quiet, the great peace of a king slaughtered. What would the world be like if men never ruled again?

She has let the fire fall and will never stoke it, simmering the king and ram. Heavy sop of his head and hair, pushed down to the bottom, held in place with the paddle, as if he might come up for breath and must be prevented.

Voices outside, some new disturbance, and Jason appears. White ghost come from some other realm, from the mountains of her home, peaks of snow. Cold breath of him, stone heart.

I have made you king, Medea says. Take what is yours from Acastus.

Where is Pelias?

In the stew, chopped into pieces by his daughters, trying to make him young.

What have you done, Medea?

Are you Acastus? Those were his words. Take your throne. Wait until the sun is coming, so they know Pelias has not returned, then claim what was taken from your father.

Jason steps closer, looks down to see his feet in ash and blood, thick red paste turning black, steps away again. You risked our sons, he says.

Yes. I risked everything. Don't waste it.

We could have been slaughtered in our sleep.

He turns away, as he always does, leaves her. Cost of years separated, without rest, Jason and Medea foreign to each other now, and Medea can no longer remember. It may always have been this way. He joins the supplicants outside, entreating an empty moon as it falls beyond the mountains.

Last dark of Nute, only stars and cries of grief from daughters. Long night seemingly without end but then the sky has already lightened, a deep blue, and Medea waits for Jason to rise but hears nothing. She stirs the remains, fire gone but cauldron still hot. The sky pales, Jason as weak as his father, not claiming his birthright, so Medea throws the paddle to the ground, steps outside, leaves this room forever.

Iolcans, she yells. Pelias the thief, untrue king, without birthright, has been hacked into pieces by his daughters. Peisidike said she would make him young, as she did for the old ram, but apparently she wanted her father dead. Tyrant king, loved by no one, not even his daughters. So now you have a true king restored, Jason, son of Aeson, whose throne was stolen.

A hundred voices at once, everyone rising from the ground. Terror in all, because all need to be ruled. It is not possible to live without a king. No one wants a moment like this, the world unordered. They would put a goat on the throne before they'd leave the throne empty.

Jason light blue at dawn, the white dust of marble transformed. He looks like a god, cut from the air, emanating his own light. He raises his thick arms, shaped by the quarry, and finally there is only one other voice, Acastus, thin whining demanding the guards kill, but no voice of a king, and the guards wait, for now.

My father was king, Jason says. Murdered by his brother after seeing his wife and younger son also murdered. Acastus is stained in that blood.

And you are stained in my father's blood, Acastus yells, murdered by your barbarian wife.

Jason lets his arms fall and watches Medea. All have gone silent. The sky brightening, her grandfather climbing the far side of the world. Her fate will be decided now, she knows, and not by her. Very strange. She didn't foresee this moment.

True, Jason says for all to hear. Medea blames Peisidike, but we all know the daughters of Pelias must have been tricked. Medea worships Hekate, worships night and darkness. She cut her own brother into pieces and has murdered Pelias in the same way. This is my barbarian wife, covered in blood. If the people of Iolcus tell us to leave, we will leave.

Voices everywhere, eruption like birds on an island, rookery without wings. These people just as stupid as birds, flaring up and veering as a group, settling again, then rising. Anyone could rule them, but she has restored true birthright, given the one destined to be king, and for this he has betrayed her. Father of her children, the man for whom she killed her own brother and left everything.

Statue cut from stone, a man without blood, without pulse, without feeling. He stands watching her as the birds circle. Medea and Jason the only two still points, all else in motion. All will happen too quickly. All her work will be undone. And there's nothing she can do, betrayed so completely.

Acastus is gathering men, his father's guards, surrounded by spear points. Jason only waits. Something in him not meant to rule. He willed this moment. He wants to be outcast.

Sky white and burning, the sun nearly risen. Medea must go to her children. But she's looking for Asteropeia, the only one true. Swallowed somewhere in this crowd. Voices rising, saying the name of Acastus, choosing slavery again. The comfort of spear and throne and all ordered as it was. She will never see Asteropeia again.

Medea runs for her children, away from this crowd, through stone streets abandoned and foreign, city that could have been hers. She expects to find them killed, throats slit, left to bleed out in the dirt. If there is enough of Pelias in Acastus, this will have been done already.

Hillside of hovels, home for years, endured for nothing, her life held in suspension, whipped and burned and wasted, and she knows she will find her children slaughtered but runs toward them anyway. Is there any choice?

Homes like urns, not much larger, mud and stick. She weaves between them, slows as she comes close. No movement, no living being, no sound here. She stands before her cave hole and knows that all the kings in the world cut into pieces and cooked will not be enough to make up for this.

There is no air to breathe. She kneels and crawls into darkness and reaches for bodies. Warm, still warm, and she feels movement, sobs as she feels each part of them, checks each arm and leg and head to find all intact and no blood. My babies, she says.

We're not supposed to talk, they tell her. We're not supposed to move.

Yes, she says. Hurry. And she pulls them from shadow as the first sun cuts through the olive grove on the slope above, turning each tiny leaf to pale gold. We have to run. Keep the sun at your back, and don't stop.

Down through other hovels, along dirt tracks away from the citadel, the world jolting, shaken, she pulls her small sons off their feet, drags until they run again, ignores their cries. She doesn't look at them, only clamps down hard on thin arms. Thistle and all else that would tear and scratch grown along the path, not wide enough for three, her children screaming at her now, but she doesn't care. They'll survive a few scratches. She has gone beyond blood and

breath and muscle, runs from some other source, untiring. The gods must feel this, the earth spread beneath and
passing without effort, distance collapsed. She has grown
taller, her limbs stretching, feet no longer touching ground,
as weightless as shadow.

Nothing grows here without thorn or spike. Ground of stone white and red and black, veins raised up in endless small ridges crumbling, backs of beasts buried long ago, earth-giants looking downward. In the distance, combined, all somehow looks brown, broken mountains baked. All that grows keeps low, vines without green, pale discs burnt and still alive, catching at her sons as she drags them along. Even the tufts of yellow grass have spikes in their seeds.

Every settlement ends this way, in wilderness abrupt and complete, place of wind and beast and the gods. No olive or fig or grape. But Acastus will follow.

Looking over her shoulder as she runs, for spear and shield and dust, listening for feet. Hekate, she calls. Let every beast of rock and earth rise up in their path. Make us unfound. Lose us in a wasteland.

She runs and runs toward nothing, her shadow slipping closer, shifting over that ground, shrinking. No longer any cries from her sons, stumbling weight she pulls along. No longer weightless herself but stiffening, legs rigid and painful, throat torn.

If she stops, they'll be killed, but finally her legs lock and she's standing in place directly under the sun on earth white and blinding. She drops the arms of her sons, looks down to see her hands covered in blood. The skin just above their wrists torn and bleeding but not cut deep.

They lie unmoving on the ground, curled inward like two seeds, but she can see them breathing hard.

Shade, she says. We need trees. And water.

Open raised valley between hills, no water in sight, but at the base of one hill, a cut of small pines. She pulls her sons to their feet, tells them to follow, staggers toward shade.

Grove in a desert, receding, farther away than it looks, long twisting path through low scrub and rock, the earth never smooth, even the air thickening to slow them, but they do reach the trees and lie down in pine straw. Sun directly overhead, so they hide close to the trunks, burrowed in, and Medea watches the path from Iolcus.

Ashen spears and shields, same in every land, all unthinking, blind power of men. She expects them to appear at any moment, unstoppable, without need of water or rest or reason except command. Medea has never had an army. She has always had to work alone. No less effective in killing a king, but still, what was it like for Hatshepsut, long ago, to command an army, thousands of men, and a navy? She built her ships on the Nile, then her men took them apart, piece by piece, and carried over the desert to reassemble at the sea and sail to the land of Punt. Ships as large as the Argo. What was it to know that power?

Hatshepsut without children, without weakness. Wearing her beard, untouchable, and further back in time, closer to the gods and origins, but also alone.

Medea keeps a hand on Aeson, her older son, named for Jason's father. His face scratched now, thin red lines and the flesh swelling pink on either side. Hair uncut, slave unwashed, but that has ended. He looks like Jason, but unimaginably soft. She crawls closer to put her lips in the hollow between eye and nose, perfect hollow. Her first baby. Scent of him, still new. And when he's grown into a man?

Medea closes her eyes, keeps her lips against his skin, and falls closer and closer, her foot over her younger son, the three of them alone in oblivion. They won't be taken from her, flesh of her flesh, the only kingdom she owns. She will lead them through wilderness, cross this desert, until they can find some new place to form new lives. Whether Jason will be there, she doesn't know. Untrue, betrayer, no father or husband.

When she wakes, the shadows have stretched back toward Iolcus, air still and hot. Large grasshoppers like sentinels all around, rigid, waiting to be flung. Large dark eyes without centers, voids, bodies woven from grass, here now and then gone.

No soldiers on the path, no traders or travelers, all empty beneath the sky. But Medea waits. They can't outrun an army. They can only hide and spend the night here, and if tomorrow there is still no sign of Acastus or his men, she'll know they're safe.

Acastus as king. She would like to return with her own army and scatter every stone of Iolcus until it looks no different from any other hillside and there is no sign left. She would erase even the memory of Pelias, and all his descendants. If not for Jason, she could have done that. Made slaves for six years, then he hands the throne to the son.

He appears on the path far away as if summoned by her thoughts. Jason carrying twin sacks tied around his shoulders, hanging in front. Still dusted white. Bulked shadow, blight on the land, solitary traveler, and she considers not calling out to him. Her sons asleep. Hidden in this grove far to the side. She could watch him pass and never see him again. Is there anything that binds, anything left beyond history and obligation? Untrue heart that would leave her alone and feel nothing. He would let her pass and not call out. My barbarian wife, covered in blood. His words.

So she would let him pass. But he's walking heavily under those sacks. He'll have food and water, and though she can do without, her sons cannot. Jason, she calls, and all other forms her life might have taken vanish. This moment locks her again into a future with him, and who can say what that will be?

Aeson rouses from her yell, and Promachus, too. He should not have been named for Jason's murdered younger brother. Nothing that has been done can be undone, and the gods should not be reminded.

Jason stops, head alert, tries to gauge direction. Small and far away still, open flats curving upward into hills, shaped by some hand enormous, abandoned since. Very little green, few trees, all visible and exposed, but her voice hidden. He turns to one side then another, searching, and even now, if she doesn't call again, some other life might still be hers.

Aeson and Promachus too tired to rise for their father. But Medea, slave to these sons, calls Jason, stands and steps clear of the trees.

No answering call, but he sees her. It will be the four of them now. This will be the first day they ever spend together. Life they might have had.

Jason careful with the sacks when he arrives, bending and tilting to lay first one on the ground and then the other. His skin wet.

Is Acastus following? Medea asks.

No.

Why not?

He's afraid of you. All will fear you, always, and we will never have lives.

That fear was your chance. Do you think any king has ever ruled without fear?

You know nothing about kings.

Medea laughs. I know nothing about kings. Stupid barbarian, woman-animal.

Jason doesn't answer. He takes a goatskin from one of the sacks, tips back water, offers none to her.

That city was mine, Medea says. You have taken away the city I won.

Jason looks back toward Iolcus, away from her, mute. His arms streaked, small brown rivers removing the white silt of stone, his skin of the past six years washing away.

You were a slave, Medea says. You would have been a slave the rest of your life, and your sons, too. All that you owe me is becoming too large. Brother, father, family, home, golden fleece, the Thracians who would have overtaken, the death of Pelias who made you a slave. Our sons, royal heirs to all the kingdoms you refuse. How will you repay?

You have drowned everything in blood. Blood can be repaid in only one way. Your death will be a vengeance by all the gods greater than Hekate. They will scatter pieces of you to every corner of the world. They will do what you did to your brother and Pelias, but there will be a thousand pieces. And no one will mourn you.

Medea smiles. What gods? Where is Poseidon? The great waves Pelias promised, to wash us all away. And Athena, builder and protector of nothing. You stole your ship from the Egyptians. Your gods are mewling wet things without eyes.

Jason puts his hands over his ears. Enough.

Korinth. Jason says they are going to Korinth. The next city where he will not be king. Track that could be leading anywhere, night spent on the ground with snakes.

Sky without cloud, without shelter. She and Jason and their sons mute and stumbling along until they fall from hills into a great long valley. Shadow along its hidden edge, long trough running toward the sea.

This way, Jason says. Soaked in sweat, carrying the sacks of water and food. Kreon knows me, knew my father, knows generosity to friends. We'll be welcome in his home.

Maybe we can be slaves, Medea says.

Jason continues down the path.

I like being whipped, Medea says, and Aeson and Promachus are old enough now. Their hands can harden to any task.

Valley that extends beyond sight, the world growing again. How many of these places exist without her?

Sun falling, a day of exile ending. Feet blistered and raw, her sons limping. Strange peace. A light breeze in evening, the air cooling. It might be better if they never reach another city. The four of them only, wandering across the earth, walking farther each day until there is no speech or thought, only movement. This might be how she and Jason could know each other and no longer betray.

They spend the night under oak trees near a dry streambed. Leaves like small hands blotted against a darkening sky. Lobed hands, silent, black on blue, a multitude. Her sons pushing in close. She lies on her back with her arms around them, their heads on her breasts. To spend the entire night together like this is a gift she had never imagined possible. To hear them breathe and feel their tugs and kicks in sleep, burrowing in deeper.

Jason a shadow somewhere else on this ground, separate.

Trees looming above thick like a second surface, and stars filling every gap, traces of a great golden fleece hung unreachable, known imperfectly from below. All that one could ever dream of is here. Body of Nute, without end.

The next day, Jason ranges far ahead, even with the burden of his sacks. Valley floor, dry yellow grass, occasional oaks, and this lone figure bare under the sun receding. Something in him that would never stop but only keep walking, toward nowhere. Lost husband, lost father. Medea doesn't know what would bring him back. Nothing in her, certainly.

Empty world same as when it began, unchanged, without time. Medea and her two sons might be waiting a thousand years before Hatshepsut will be born. No sign, nothing to give reference.

Aeson and Promachus, names used again, lives returned and repeated. Names that would take away more than they would give, her sons burdened by ancestors. She doesn't know why she allowed this, but perhaps because she had no ancestors at all herself, beyond her father, and missed their weight. Some comfort in reaching back, some assurance, but these were unfinished lives, cut short, and won't they demand something still?

Shape of her sons' lives unknown. Released now from slavery, begun again. Remnants of Aeetes, walking in a foreign land, and will they ever see Colchis? Is it possible to be from a place one has never seen?

They walk this long valley for three days, staying away from settlements, avoiding all other humans. Medea has too much time to think of great Aeetes. Endless valley, sound of her own footsteps lost in the steps of these two sons, and she has spread his seed, serves him still. Heirs in another kingdom, his influence widening. How can she end all kings when she has carried them within her, betrayed by her own womb? Can any king ever be killed? Pelias, too, lives on through Acastus and so many daughters. His heirs will multiply. He will never be fully erased.

Each night, though, she lies with Aeson and Promachus pulled close, pieces of her own body, and can't imagine the world without them. As necessary as moon and sun and water, and not belonging to her father. Reclaimed in darkness, belonging only to her.

Cyzicus left no heirs. Does he remember the feel of Medea's body on his, first embrace after death? Does he long for her? Shadows, each of us living in multiple forms. Medea's body is with Jason wherever he lies on this ground, and with Cyzicus, and with her sons, and with Asteropeia, perhaps even Aeetes, and also alone. The gods will demand something too, each of us lying down with Nute each night, and Hekate's arms reaching up from below.

Valley in which one might wander forever, sealed away from Iolcus and Korinth. Small streams falling from dry mountains, bare trickles enough to refill the sacks of water. Jason hanging back to let them drink and eat, then walking ahead again, mute fragment of earth. Rejoining at night to sleep, gone at first light.

Hills in the distance, hung before them unreachable, folds in the air. Without roots, no connection to the valley floor, lost somewhere in waves of heat. At the edge of where gods dive through land to keep it from dissolving into nothing, margins left imperfect, unformed. All hardening beneath Medea's feet.

Her younger son falling behind, so she carries him on her back, his mouth on her neck, wet as he loses himself in sleep. Weight of him slumped, hills gaining color, deepening into brown and even red, smooth slopes become sharp, outcrops of rock and the valley rising, tilting.

They climb in shadow, Aeson before her, Promachus on her neck, leave the valley and find Jason in last light as if he were a remnant god, not yet fled.

Your sons are still alive, she says.

He has left the sacks on the ground, goatskins of water, the last of the food. Salted fish, dried meat, all that makes the tongue burn.

We're not far now, he says. Two or three days. Through these hills and another valley, shorter, and a few more hills.

What will we eat?

I'll kill something, he says. Or we'll just wait. It's only two or three days. We have water.

And who could want more than that?

In Korinth, we'll have plenty.

Depending on Kreon. We certainly received a great welcome from Pelias. You handed over the fleece and all was laid at our feet.

Jason doesn't argue. He only turns away, something in him resigned. Enough light still to watch his back as he goes. Appearing from the mist in Colchis, her new life, and disappearing now. She doesn't know how to bring him back. She feels as if she herself is the one disappearing, losing weight and substance, being erased, hung in the air to feel loss and nothing more, some vague emptiness that is no longer painful but only true.

She lies on this ground as it cools, pulls her sons close. They will keep her from vanishing. Anchors to this world.

Narrow land, isthmus between seas come so close to meeting. The familiar one pale and whipped white by wind, the new one dark, much deeper, and sheltered.

A great mountain, rocky head thrust up to watch over Korinth. Some elder, outcrops of rock like a fringe of hair. Man, not woman. We should not go here, she tells Jason.

Kreon is a friend, Jason says. Friend of my father.

The air whited beneath blue, wind cooler, and from this hilltop they might turn any direction, set a new path. They could go along the shore of this new sea. But Jason steps down the bare slope and her sons follow, starving, wanting food.

Medea follows because what else can she do? Her feet not touching ground, dizzy. Settlement at the base of that rocky head, small city of stone. The same mud huts spread over flatland, and one of these hovels will be their new home. Arriving in slave's clothing, filthy and desperate.

All stare as they pass. With every traveler, some new story begins. The only thing their arrival cannot mean is nothing.

Fertile here, groves of olive, shade of fig, grapes low along the ground. Springs from this mountain. A fortunate place, potters with water for their work, large urns painted, a wealthy place. Fishermen, also, close enough to the sea, and farmers and shepherds. Bronze workers tending their fires in bright day. Weavers and spinners and masons, and as they near the citadel and the group of houses built in stone, signs everywhere of visitors from other lands, from Egypt and Minoa and Thracia, cloth and glass and metal foreign and rich. From that new sea, also, there must come peoples Medea cannot name, and from elsewhere on this rumored peninsula, Mycenae and Argos and many more. The poverty of Iolcus even more apparent now.

Streets no longer of dirt but of stone, and their arrival noticed, spearmen appearing, king's guards. Narrow alleys, a maze easily defended. Medea keeps her sons close, a hand on each one's neck as they walk before her. Jason the slave, broad backed, sacks left behind, walking past the soldiers as if they aren't worth notice.

Medea would snap each of these men in two, break these walls and burn all that will burn. Another king. Grown somehow in limitless number all across the world. In each new place, some new tyrant, and why no other form of rule?

She will be made anything today, slave or whore or friend of the king, with slaves beneath her. She will be killed or whipped or bathed and dressed and honored with a feast, all at the whim of one man she has never met, and she has no say over what will happen to her children.

Long shadow of the mountain above, that rocky head. No accident the king is approached in this direction. Weight and presence and fear. All that Jason refuses to learn.

Guards close now. Through a narrow entrance opens a large courtyard and, beyond that, massive stones for the throne room. Somewhere inside this other king, same as Pelias.

They step through shadow, find a realm lit from above, four pillars and open center to the roof, raised hearth. Flat slab larger than the hearth of Pelias. Sacrificial stone, and she imagines her sons placed on that altar.

Jason, Kreon calls. Son of my friend Aeson.

Appearing from shadow in a great robe of gold, embracing Jason. Closing his eyes in pleasure. Guards on every side.

Graybeard king welcoming home what could be a lost son. How did Pelias let you go? he asks. I heard he kept you as a slave, and you wear the clothing of a slave.

Pelias is dead, Jason says.

I killed him, Medea says. I am Jason's barbarian wife, covered in blood. Jason's words. Iolcus was his, and he left it to Acastus. The tyrant Pelias, false king, was killed by his own daughters, cut up into a stew.

Kreon drops his arms from around Jason. What do you bring here?

Medea.

Is Acastus behind you with his army?

No.

And Pelias butchered by his own daughters?

Yes.

But how?

They cut up an old ram, and Medea made a lamb appear.

Peisidike made a lamb appear.

Medea bent the world and made the daughters of Pelias see strangely. They cut up their own father with axes and believed he could be made young.

Medea, Kreon says. You cut your own brother into pieces.

Yes.

You are not welcome here, Medea. You may stay with your sons because Jason is welcome. But you will not speak to my daughter. You will not be alone with her. And you will not walk at night. If my guards find you at night anywhere but your own bed, you will be killed.

Coward-king, Medea says. Afraid of the dark.

Take her away before I kill the wife of Jason, Kreon tells his guards.

Be careful not to sleep, Medea says as guards take her arms. Touch my sons and I boil you alive. Another king in a stew.

Medea! Jason yells. Kreon welcomes us into his home. Welcomes you.

Guards pull her away and her sons follow, instinct in them. They will always follow their mother.

She's not taken far. No mud hut at the edge of Korinth. Royal room, walls painted with hunts and battles and women. Chariots, though what chariot has ever been here in Korinth, driven on what road? Echoes of Egypt. These people unable to imagine themselves, seeing only the pharaohs.

A royal couch, lined in lamb's wool. She sits her sons here, kneels before them. Listen, she says, and she touches their faces, traces the shape of them. Skin softer than lamb's wool, eyes large pools unending, deep brown without surface, color of caves, Jason's eyes, not the gray of her own or her father's. They will try to take you away from me.

Aeson looking into her eyes bravely, remnant of a lost king, heir to another. How many kings in him? Blood of how many tyrants?

I am the only one who loves you, she tells her sons. I am the only one.

She rises and takes their hands, leads them to the large bed. Lies down on her back and they come to her, rest their cheeks on her breasts, and she wraps her arms around. Their legs intertwined with hers, roots grown together. Let Kreon try to separate them.

A feast that night for the hero-slave. Triumphant return for a son who never left and is not a son. Medea seated far away, corner of the courtyard with Aeson and Promachus. Vines along stone walls, and she's been buried here, separated from Jason. Guards with torches standing to either side, as if they are only providing light.

Jason held close between Kreon and his daughter, Glauce, who stretches her neck and tilts and coos and studies his arms and eyes and mouth. Young, very young, hardly more than a girl, and never made a slave or mother. Her only concern is ornament. Glancing at her own wrists, at gold bracelets, how they fall, folds of thin Egyptian cloth over her breasts. If her breasts were cauldrons, she would fall in, drawn by her limitless desire for herself, and Jason would fall with her. He speaks with Kreon and never sees him, sees only young flesh.

Aeson and Promachus devouring meat. Sounds of their mashing. Eyes for nothing more than their food, unaware of all that is changing. Ramming their faces into hot flesh, their mouths not big enough.

Medea is starving, but she cannot eat. Forced to watch this show without sound, without words, too far, only gestures and glances, and Jason doesn't look her way, not even once. Barbarian wife, too much trouble, left behind now. Somehow she didn't believe this would happen. They were tied together with wet rope, bound and crushed in the sun.

All happening so quickly, everything changed in a single day. Years of slavery, days unnumbered, lost as nothing, slow separation but not final, and now everything slips in an instant. Something in Jason waiting for this.

Women of Korinth, wealthy, watching her but looking away, refusing to catch her eye. They all know what's happening. Every person in this courtyard, even the men, and every servant, every guard, all know that Jason is being taken from her and that she's being forced to watch. Glauce the center of all desire, Medea outcast. Both daughters of kings, but Colchis far away, not only in distance but also in time and event. No return possible.

Women, Medea says, just loud enough for the nearest tables to hear. Women with children, how can you watch?

They continue to eat, obscene feast, dressed as Egyptians, headdresses falling in bars of black and gold, finely turned cups of wine, fingers thick with rings. Animals pretending

to be gods, daughters of shepherds aping royalty. The luck
of a crossroads, city of two seas.

Even gold can burn, Medea says.

They can hear. They don't respond, but she knows they
can hear.

A guard takes her arm, makes her stand. She could howl
now, scream and accuse Jason, remind him of all he's promised and all she's sacrificed, but she remains silent. Something darker working in her, some rage that refuses anything
as slight as words. Led back to her room with Aeson and
Promachus, left alone to lie in darkness and form waking
dreams of revenge.

Sound of the feast, laughter for hours. Stringed lute and
hand drums, dancing and clapping. Jason freed, holding the
hand of this girl-child. Medea can see her small mouth, waiting, scent of her bathed in cinnamon, no slave. Their children
will inherit Korinth and have a claim, also, to Iolcus, surrounding Athens. Kreon's dreams, but Jason will want only
that ripe young body and release from a wife who has been
difficult from the first.

Night without end. Rise and fall of breath, her sons' hearts
beating beneath her hands, feel of their ribs. Her own body
engorging, filling with hate and hollowed, void under pressure
increasing in her head and chest, unfairness so enormous nothing can be done. Jason does not return. Sounds dying away, no
more music, no more shouts, quiet of night, and still no husband
but gone to another bed. Medea's breath fast, in panic, though
she only lies here holding her sons. Glauce in some royal bed
very close, only a few arm's lengths away, lit in torchlight, bar-
ing herself for Jason, spreading her legs, untorn by children.

Or perhaps they're not allowed that yet. Perhaps they linger at some gate of stone, some corner in shadow, and bend toward each other, wanting to devour, held back, what she felt for Asteropeia. Jason with his fist in Glauce's hair, biting her neck, feeling his spine. Medea replaced, all desire for her gone, no thought of his children, no thought of consequence. Because what will happen now?

Men never think of consequence. Given too much, and they believe all will be given still. But Medea knows, even in her rage, that she will take him back. When he returns and begs, what choice will she have? Father of her children, and all she has, alone, an outcast, unwelcome here.

They will leave, walk back toward Athens, perhaps, somewhere beyond the base of that long valley. A friend of hers, King Aegeus. She should have insisted they flee to Athens, not Korinth. Aegeus knew her father. Another king without a son, like Kreon, but an older king, softened over time. And no friend of Kreon's. No bordering kings ever friends. He will favor her over Jason, has no daughter to offer. Something in him likes Hekate, knows darkness and despair and loneliness and older gods born from earth. Older world in him, someone who knew the previous king of the Hittites and a different pharaoh in Egypt.

He visited her temple to Hekate, at night surrounded by fires, came alone and wanted her. Old man and desire that he will not forget, no one to answer to and nothing left to lose in his final days. Athens more powerful than Korinth, and she will find shelter there.

Jason never does return. Helios appearing, pale light of Medea's defeat. Husband lost, all sacrifices made for nothing.

Something in her still believes he will cross that threshold, come in and kneel before her. Her willingness to forgive him, to take him back, how could that not be used?

Can one night mean so much?

Aeson and Promachus rouse in the light, push and grab as they wake, yawn and flop against her, innocent. To them, an easier night than any before. Easiest night of their lives. Feast and a comfortable bed, their mother to themselves. No mud hut, no sleeping on the ground or on goat hair. Waking in a new place to explore, no longer slaves. Hungry, and slaves are listening outside, appear through the door at the first sounds, bring figs and honey, bread and cheese and milk, set a feast on a long table against the wall.

Her sons laughing, smearing honey on each other's faces as they devour. Calling for her to join, so she rises and sits beside them, chews a piece of bread, her jaws flat and slack, far away, some beast in the field and nothing more, dumb creature without thought, but they tug at her and make her try figs and even dates, large and too sweet, brought from somewhere over the sea. They paint her face, too, with the honey, and she should laugh and smile but she feels dead.

What should a mother want? Her sons happy, her husband in favor with the king. After so many years of labor in stone and fire, a release. All given to them, easy lives. She should learn to bow down, forget Jason's vows, forget all she sacrificed, and be grateful. Let him return when he wants, go away when he pleases, ask no questions, apologize to Kreon for her rough words. Isn't this what a mother should do?

How, then, can she make herself do this? Hekate, she calls. Or softer Nute. Tell me how.

Medea walks without blood. Nothing in her veins but air, no organs, hollowed chest. Aeson and Promachus some-where at play, freed. Walk of the dead, and this must be what it feels like afterward. Severed from all but still walking. Street of rock ground into whited dust. Windy here, whorls in the air. Shade trees bending. Vendors with black skin and baskets of dates shiny golden brown, slick with sugar. Baskets in the shapes of amphoras, as if all things could be repeated in different material, a person made of clay or reed or stone or water.

Narrow street full of sound. Humans come to fill the air, to make no place quiet. Hands reaching for her, holding

DAVID VANN

shapes of root and leaf and orb. Bright colors, red and yellow
and green, all without meaning. Strange dismemberments,
objects without origin or use. Sound the same, in its own
shapes severed and hung unrecognized. Tongues she has never
heard. Smells brought together too close, undistinguished.

Small figures in clay, painted in lines red and black. Bulls
with wide thin horns, bodies narrowed impossibly like dogs.
Standing alert, no heaviness of a bull, no long sideways swing
of a head. Figures on thrones, for all to imagine themselves
kings. Thrones rounded like baskets, and each king's head as
tiny as a bird's. Mothers fattened. Faces with opened mouths
screaming. Rams with heads thickening.

Women offered for burial, arms become wings upspread,
beaked faces, rounded breasts. Women meant for graves.
Standing in crowds before her, waiting.

Bronze in hoops and rings and bracelets, trace of each tiny
dent and bending and hammer blow, sign of all that is human,
shaping figures from nothing, remaking the world. Forms
imagined and repeated without end.

Herbs and remedies hung in baskets, dried root and bulb,
roots black and still carrying earth, flowers and then one
that would stop everything. A flower she has seen before,
serpent skin petals in purple and white, pattern to confuse, so exactly like snakeskin, but this brilliant color. Black
seeds to divert the eye as the petals come closer, long and
tapered and reaching. Burial from when the earth was first
made, when light and color and form were not yet decided,
forgotten and risen now without resemblance or corollary, without place or name or belonging. Eruption of the
same material from which gods were made, not meant for

humans, nursed on poison. The large bulb from which it rises each autumn more poisonous in its flesh than any other plant Medea knows. Its blood was what she used to protect Jason from the bulls, afraid it might burn his skin, but it poisons only the inside, and the bulls would not breathe it, turned their heads away.

A dozen of these flowers and their bulbs waiting before her so unlikely, strange recognition, pattern in a life, fate we can never outrun. All the distance she has traveled from Colchis across three seas to Iolcus and through valleys and hills here to Korinth, all the years passed, and on this day, here as she wanders almost without sight, so lost, she ends up standing before crocus that might protect or heal but has another use. Crocus that would shed any name and remain only what it is, color and pattern that would end thought, sign of an unsolid world.

Beautiful, Medea says, and the old woman selling them doesn't smile. I'll take them all.

The slaves following Medea pick up the flowers and bulbs carefully, holding them away at arm's length, some instinct.

Medea strolls in the sun and wind, restored, present again. Some fear of Kreon's guards, but what would they see? Only flowers. And she has made no plan. She was not looking for crocus. She takes one from a slave and cups it in her hands, walks among the women of Korinth, lets the bright petals brush arms and backs. Soft touch almost unnoticed, softer than any lover's. Women of Korinth, Medea whispers. Do I not have a right, some right to punish my husband? Did he not make vows? I have no one here, no family, no friend. He takes away all.

These women ignore her. She passes close enough to touch and they refuse to notice. They pick up a bracelet or admire an urn or whisper in another's ear. Everyone here aware of only one person, Medea, sensing her every movement, but with no recognition. Body without weight, leaving no shadow. Fallen wife, usurped and left an outcast.

Plain bulb in her hands, same as for any other flower, but holding a liquid that would loosen everything inside. Medea tried only a small amount in Colchis. At night, alone, in Hekate's temple, wanting to learn the use of each root and bulb and growth.

Nothing at first. She waited and became sleepy, thought it must have been the wrong flower, then woke with her mouth and throat burning. Dry flame. Water had no hold, passed her throat without effect. Then the burning moved lower, deep in her bowels, and everything fell from her, all liquid, more than seemed possible. She threw up until she could offer only a thin red drool, lay curled on stone in her foul mess fevered and sweating, even her eyes leaking, as all turned to mush inside her, even her lungs, unable to breathe, and all felt not like water but like flame melting.

She could not straighten, could not stand. Deep cramp and pain in pattern like the serpent skin of these petals, always moving, impossible to locate, exquisite and beautiful pain unlike any she'd felt before or since, an excess beyond what she could recognize, and her only wish was for death.

But the poison lasted. Agony without end. When daylight came, she crawled away from stone across fallen leaves gold and red and yellow, mosaic of the forest floor. Veins of each leaf raised and pulsing, slack mottled skin sagging, rough hide, fevered visions as she crawled across the back of some great beast. Feeling the heat of it below cold air. A breeze and shadow, her body shivering and still leaking, draining away behind her, and she began to think the air was the poison, because her lungs were rotting. She tried not to breathe.

Platelets of skin as large as her hand. She worried what might emerge at the edges, from the cracks, between the yellow and red, wanted to stand and run. She would have died, easily, of thirst as all water left her, or of chill as night came, drenched in sweat, but she was found somehow, rescued, carried to the citadel where water was poured inside and she was like a river, passing liquid in torrents and sudden gushes. Four days of fever and burning, and on the fifth, when it subsided, when she was able, finally, to hold water and even small bits of food, she was still too weak to stand, but in another two days she was walking.

She never told the cause. All believed her consumed by a malign god, price of worshipping Hekate, and this suited her power. Feared by all, because was this god still in her? Was she Medea or something else? But here in Korinth, all think she is nothing more than a spurned wife, unhappy woman. They believe she can be ignored. They think her pain will have no consequence. They think they are safe.

In her room, Medea arranges these flowers on the long table, curling nest of snakes in the air, pure white encased in light purple as if the tint were netting, as if these petals were the capture of something. Black seeds a hundred small eyes, unnoticed at first, but so dark they refuse place, hang separate from the soft flesh of the flower.

When her sons rush in, she tells them not to touch. They lean as close as they can, their faces near, grubby hands on the table twisting toward bulb and stem.

Get out, she says. Stay away from those. She pushes them out the door and they run off shouting in some new game. Jason's arm around her, that's what she would like, the two of them watching their sons play, then going inside. This beautiful room, beautiful city, no longer slaves. If Jason were true, this would be the good time of their lives, the easy time. Simple.

Medea lies down to rest, exhausted somehow, and when she wakes, it's almost dark, the sun fallen. She's alone and caged here, not allowed to walk at night. She's missed the rest of her day. And where are her children?

The moment she rises, slaves bring in food. They've been waiting, watching, everyone always watching her. Where are my sons? she asks.

We'll bring them, she's told.

A small table for the food, the larger one given over to the crocus. Medea sits and waits. Some stew of lamb, prepared by a slave standing at a cauldron, same as Medea only days ago. Change so abrupt. All gained and lost in a blink.

Stew of king and ram. Acastus waiting for it to cool, then pulling pieces of his father free, washing for burial. Clear enough the hair and head of a king, the curled horns of a ram, but what of the rest? Whose entrails, whose splintered ribs, whose chewed balls? On that floor of ash and blood, trying to decide which parts are a man.

Pelias. The king whose power was without limit. Now Kreon.

Aeson charging through the door, almost knocking her over in her chair. Slick arms, smell of sweat, hot breath, and she can feel his pulse, feel his heart beating against her. Then Promachus worming his way in, grubby and snot nosed and whining. She pulls and he burrows. Animal. Everything in human life that matters is animal and nothing more. Jason no different from any bull. Medea rutted against the same as any cow or ewe or sow, first by the male, then by the litter. This is how Medea is erased and does not become a king, no Hatshepsut.

They leave her for the food, forcing too much into their mouths, greed of children. Every child born in the nature of a king, believing itself at the center, taking all, brutal and thoughtless. Stew dripping from their mouths, loud smack of meat. Always in movement. Twisting in their chairs, heads swinging, hands grabbing and grabbing. No stillness possible. But by some cruel trick she would sacrifice all for them, would stay here in Korinth and try to forget betrayal, would live as an outcast and become nothing.

Medea forces herself to eat. Flesh of bread and lamb the same. She drinks wine to drown the taste and keeps drinking, feels her head lighten and spin and the back of her neck become so heavy she lies down, listens to the music that begins late, another feast, Jason falling into those eyes and breasts as his sons sleep. Does he think of them? Does he think of Medea? Is there anything inside him at all, or only empty space moving under momentum begun long ago, men as fate? What is Jason? What could be called Jason? How could she spend this many years with him and not know? All she knows is Medea. All others, even her sons, are voids.

Held back from the sea. She would walk to the edge and immerse, true temple of Hekate, sink down in darkness and try to understand what to do now, but the sea is farther away than before, and she's not allowed to walk in the night. Guards waiting outside her door. Another king who thinks she can be bound.

Medea doesn't sleep. Longest of nights, listening for any
sound of Glauce and Jason, feeling the spin of wine slow
and fade, leaving a terrible clarity. The air coldest just before
Helios appears, thin light of an unforgiving day, still no husband returning, and so he is never going to return.

Early morning, waiting for the air to warm and bodies
to rise. Finally Aeson and Promachus are stretching and
pushing then famished and the slaves bring in food again,
endless food. The sounds of Korinth restart and Medea
still waits.

A messenger. Jason too cowardly to come himself. A man
in her door chewing something, between smacking and swallows telling her that Jason is to marry Glauce.

But Jason is my husband, she says.

He keeps chewing, turns and walks out.

Medea is unable to move. She only stands in place before
the empty door. So soon? she asks. But she's speaking to no
one. Her sons behind her eating, unbothered.

All in Korinth have decided Medea is nothing.

Come with me, she tells her sons, and grabs their wrists
over protests and thrown food, drags them into the narrow
twisting street of stone. I don't care whether you walk or
not, she says. I'll drag you. Promachus twisting and yanking,
legs kicking, howl of that open mouth. Aeson older, smart
enough to know nothing will stop her.

Somewhere in the citadel, Jason lying in Glauce's bed, and
Medea will find this place.

Blind streets, pathways turning and leading nowhere, ending in walls. Room and wall the same, no entrances from
outside, guarded somewhere from within. Jason! she screams.

Promachus no longer dragging. Both sons stay close to save their arms.

City with no relation to ground, held somewhere in the sky suspended, and the sun spinning, rising in every direction. All meant to confuse so the king can hide, so his daughter can spread her legs and none will know. Spear points forcing her into alleys and finally trapped. She and her sons against a shaded wall too high to climb.

Jason! she screams again. I have your sons!

A dozen guards with their spears lowered. They don't move, waiting for command.

Cowards, Medea says. Dumb as brick. If Kreon told you to kill each other, you would.

Mute brick with dark blank eyes and no blood, guards made of clay and painted, line for a mouth. Power of a king, that men are no longer men. She would walk forward and shatter them against granite, but she holds a son in each hand.

Promachus afraid, starting a thin whining cry. She shakes his arm hard. No, she says. So he only cries harder, until his father appears.

Chest bare, just risen from his new bed. Sun slicing him at an angle, shoulder to hip, and he holds up a hand to shield his eyes. You, Medea, he says, then he yawns, covers his mouth, eyes closed.

You remember.

Why not rest? Why cause problems? Why scream and wake everyone?

Don't hide behind the guards. Come here.

I'm not afraid of you.

Medea smiles. You think you can marry Glauce, have new sons, replace all that came before, erase years? You forget who I am.

I know who you are, bitter woman, butcher, barbarian. I've brought you to this civilized place. I'll marry Kreon's daughter, and our sons will have royal brothers. You should thank me.

Medea cannot speak. The monstrosity too great.

Anyway, Jason says. Leave me alone. He turns to walk away.

Do you really think I'm so stupid? Medea asks. Do you think woman is made out of dust, without blood, without thought? That you can say anything, and that will be true?

Rage, Jason says. All you are is rage. You would cut every person into pieces, some practice of your brutal backward people. But not here.

Do you think a spear won't go through Kreon? Kings are the same as any other meat.

Enough.

No. Not enough at all. I am owed.

I owe you nothing.

Medea raises the hands of Aeson and Promachus. Do you see these, your sons?

Yes. Gifts I gave to you. Fortunate woman, risen above her kind. And now they will have royal brothers.

Medea would laugh if she didn't know this was the end. Consequence, she says. There is always consequence. You won't spurn me and see nothing happen. You know that's true. Search somewhere in that tiny heart of yours and remember. You've known me for long enough. Did Pelias escape consequence? I don't want what will happen next, and neither do you. Stop it here. Come back to me and to these sons named after your father and brother. Leave Glauce.

Be grateful, Jason says. A woman is never grateful but always wants more.

He leaves her trapped at spear point against a wall with their sons. She would scream, but there's no one to hear. An entire city deaf to her.

The guards back away slowly, leave a thin corridor for her to pass. She is to return to her cage.

Dark bronze tied to sticks. Don't sleep, she says. Hekate in your dreams. You'll grab your own spear and impale yourself. And his new wife. If Glauce gives birth to a son, it will have two heads, reminder from Hekate that this is a second marriage.

Kreon at her door almost immediately. Surrounded by guards. Coward-king.

Medea, he says. You are banished. You and your sons. Leave now and never return.

His voice too high, strained. He's afraid of her. No Pelias. No belief in his power, no will to torture and break and rule. Graybeard lamb put on a throne long ago by a father. But she must play her part.

Please, she says, and drops to her knees. What have I done? Jason leaves me for your daughter, and now you banish me and my children, send us away into nothing?

You've made threats. Against me, against my daughter, against Jason. I know the monster you are, someone who would cut up her own brother. You will leave now or be killed.

Do you care so little for the gods? What of Jason's vows?

Yours was no marriage. Glauce will be his first wife.

First wife, Medea says. She falls forward in prostration, her hands and forehead to stone. This is the only way she can keep from grabbing a spear. She must control herself. She needs time.

Stone that smells of salt. Dank dust and all that is hidden in every place, dried water of every birth given in this room, shadow and scent of all who came before. Kreon and Jason forget. They think they are the first to live. They think the world is not old. Glauce, too, must think hers is the first soft flesh to rise.

Please, Medea says. You know it's not in my nature to beg. But let me have some time to arrange for my children. Banishment to me is nothing, but I must take care of my children. You are a father. You know that children must come first.

She waits, and she does not rise. Cool stone, tilt of it, Kreon standing in the air above her, unreachable. She would peel away his ribs and have him walk opened, for all to see that a king is the same inside as any other man, have him walk until so much dust clings to every organ he simply stops and is not able to take another step. So many ways to kill a king, and each must be tried.

Well, Kreon says finally. Soft words. It's not in my nature to be a tyrant. We do have to think of your children. You may have until tomorrow. I shouldn't do this. I'm afraid of you, as everyone should be. But you can't do anything in one day. You leave in the morning.

Medea hides her smile against stone. Stupid king. Leftovers of too many generations. Thank you, she says, in what she hopes sounds like gratitude rather than triumph.

She remains face hidden until their footsteps have gone, then she rises and calls in her slaves, three women. None dare look at her.

A dress and diadem, she says. For the princess. Gifts she can wear to bed with my husband. We have to go quickly and find the very best. And then we will make sweets for her to nibble on between rutting. If only I could be there to hand them to her and smooth the sheets and make all comfortable. One of you, bring honey and flour and water, and stones to grind the bulbs of those flowers. Bring cinnamon. Bring something to strain the liquid.

Her sons are watching her. Jason's eyes. You will meet the princess today, she says. You will bring her sweets and gifts. Stay close to me now.

She leaves with her children and two of the slaves. Gold, she says. Bring me to the finest worker of gold.

The morning sun itself is golden, white dust of the market come alive in warmth and color. Sky brilliant blue. Clear fall day, cool and bright, last gift of Helios, as if to make amends. She may die today and never have to watch his transit again. A relief to that.

Wealthy women of Korinth not yet risen. Only slaves at this hour, and the house of the gold worker closed. We'll have to come back, Medea's slaves tell her.

No. Go inside and wake him.

Low door of stone, lintel crooked, dark cave, but her slave returns with a white-haired man who complains.

This is for the princess Glauce. A diadem of gold. You can name any price. But I need it now. I can't wait.

I don't have something like that, he says. Pinched face from peering too closely, fingers burned from metal. I have only funeral diadems.

That will work, Medea says and smiles. Let me see.

He's gone too long, but when he emerges, he holds a hundred suns, small beaten orbs wreathed in flame, Glauce's mouth and throat as she burns from inside, immolation. Strips of suns in dagger points like the petals of the crocus, slender and beautiful and deadly. Perfect for the new bride, Medea says.

Who will pay? he asks.

Jason. Jason will pay.

Dresses, then, smoothest and softest for that wanted skin, something to caress and encase as she burns. The slaves have to wake dressmakers. Too many in Korinth sleeping, no one aware of what today will be. Then Medea sees a man in the open-air market, an Egyptian with his bundles.

He watches her approach, seems to know to fear, says nothing.

For the princess, Medea says. Finest from Egypt. Gold in it. Let her be a pharaoh's daughter, not the daughter of a lowly weak king.

The man unties a bundle, smooth fingers, quick, sorts through half his pile and pulls free a gown of pure white with a collar and sash of gold. Feel, he says. With your fingers and with your cheek.

Medea holds the fabric in her hand, brings it to her face. I remember this, she says. From Iolcus. Alcestis had a dress as soft as this. What is it?

Linen.

Linen is not this soft.

Linen from very young flax, and treated like a princess. Woven very fine. It weighs half what these other dresses weigh, and costs four times as much. Collar and sash are a separate price.

Cloth as soft as Glauce, thin enough her breasts will be just visible beneath, shadow and desire. Over her arms, the material even thinner, in bands that will move like waves. And the collar, wide hemisphere of woven gold, sun god worshipped in every land with different names. Glauce will feel its heat. Heavy as her lungs melt. The sash binding her below, rope of gold. Glauce will not understand. The world given to her always, loved by all, belonging, poison not possible, pain not possible. She will be admiring herself right up until she feels the flames.

Jason will pay, Medea says. You may collect this evening after the gift is given.

The man only nods. Something in him understands, perhaps, that he will never be paid, but what can he say? He is an exile, same as Medea, on borrowed ground.

Lavender flesh so soft and impossible, no surface to it, no underside, patterned through. True flower. She would have this flesh herself, no inside and outside, no heart, no lungs, no womb, no blood, no history or home but only pattern of color and light unending and still.

She unsheathes her knife, bronze face of a grandfather, throat of a brother, cuts flower from source, opens a grove of poison. She expects the blade to melt or hiss, but of course this poison is without sign, without scent, fire in purest, quietest form.

Bulbs plain as clods of dirt. She washes carefully in a basin, as if they are infants, pats them dry and then slices each in half, severed flesh exposed, and slices again into quarters until all before her are in pieces.

Form of a world, form of her life, endlessly repeating.

She gathers them together, nestled in close. Her slave has brought stones for mashing, mortars and pestles, and Medea likes the feel of a stone fist. Jason's heart is what she would like in her bowl. Stone phallus to smash and grind.

Make this bulb his heart, she says. Hekate, or stronger Nute, let him feel stone. Take all away from him and let him live too long, bereft and wandering.

These women beside her afraid. But let them hear. All is too late for everyone. Kreon has let her stay.

Fibrous mass submerged now in its own liquid, tainted brown from skin and earth. Sound like feet slapping into mud. But not as much liquid as she had hoped. She won't be able to use flour. She must be more direct, a drink with honey and cinnamon, but why would they accept a drink from her?

Bring stone mugs, Medea says. Ancient. I've seen them at the feast. Cups from another time. Bring three.

Aeson and Promachus sitting on the bed watching. Are you strong, Aeson? she asks. Can you carry two heavy stone mugs?

I can carry, he says.

But then Promachus is upset, about to cry, face crumpling in child idiocy.

You'll have one to carry, too, Promachus, she says. One all to yourself.

Now he's smiling, giggling, too moronic to be true, but she can't help responding. She's at the bedside, pulling them both close, Promachus tugging at her hair. Lost, and before she knows it her slave has returned with the mugs.

Dark stone, each carved from a single piece. Black with hints of red like fire, smooth and polished from innumerable hands, thin curved handles too delicate to believe. How this was shaped from stone so long ago none can say.

Medea sets two on the table, and her slave holds coarse linen over one as Medea pours. Fiber and fleck on the surface, liquid disappearing below. Medea pours a second bowl into the cloth, waits for last drops, then wrings out linen, last poison. She lifts the mug, enough poison for twenty people, the right amount for a princess or king or husband.

She strains the other two bowls into the second cup and now adds honey, slow sweet undulation. Cinnamon, strong enough to cover any scent. She stirs a drink almost invisible in dark stone. Sweet smelling, innocent.

Into the third cup, only water, honey, and cinnamon.

Bring Jason, she says. She points to the youngest of her slaves, the most afraid, the least likely to tell. And yet what would she tell? She doesn't know what these flowers are. Bring Jason. Tell him I'm sorry and I understand his new marriage is best for all of us. Tell him our sons have gifts for the princess. Hurry.

The young slave is gone, and the other two stare down at the floor. Clear away this mess, Medea says. Hide every sign of what we've made. Leave only the gifts.

Then Medea kneels before her sons. Aeson, she says. These stone cups are heavy, but you must not spill. You must bring these to the princess and to the king.

Aeson nods, gravity of children, odd acolytes to perform ritual without understanding. Mirrors of all.

And Promachus, she says. You will carry this third cup. You'll wait until Aeson is handing his cups to the princess and king, then you can drink from yours. Everyone will laugh, but you can drink, and if there's any left, you can share with your father.

Medea will leave Jason alive. She hopes he will live unnaturally long, and she will give him plenty to remember. He will live today a thousand times.

What if they want more? Aeson asks.

Medea smiles. I think it will be enough.

She rises to arrange the beautiful dress on the table, the golden funeral diadem, the two cups and the third. All signs of mashing gone, bulb and flower, mortar and pestle. The air bright with day. She must convince Jason now, become something impossible and make him believe. A test even for the stupidity of men.

Waiting. The boys fidgeting on the bed, grabbing at each other's hands. The two older slaves standing against a wall, Medea watching the door, and when Jason arrives, his mouth is already open. What is this, Medea? You've been told to leave, so leave. Leave us alone.

Strong arms, become a brute from the quarry.

Medea drops to her knees, bows her head to hide her face. You were right, Jason, she says. I'm sorry. I'm weak and give in to rage too easily, as you know. But I see now what you've done, securing a future for our sons. With royal brothers, they'll have a place. I understand that now, and I'm grateful. You've done what is right.

But you didn't understand quickly enough, Jason says. You made threats against the king and his daughter and against me, so now you've been banished, and our children with you. You've taken away what could have been theirs.

It's too late for me, Medea says. I understand that. But not for our children. Let our sons take these gifts now to Glauce and her father. A rare dress of fine linen and gold from Egypt, a diadem of beaten gold, cups of nectar the way we made in Colchis. I know I can't offer these myself, but let the children bring the gifts, and beg Glauce and Kreon to accept them. Our sons should not be with a banished mother who is nothing. They should be here with you and their new brothers.

You think Glauce doesn't already have gold and fine linen?

Please, Medea says. She's found tears, so she raises her face now for Jason to see. This is all I have to offer. Please give our sons a better life. I love them more than you can know.

Jason in his triumph. Scowling, imperious, believing he is owed all. This is his weakness. Glauce his, the kingdom his, so why shouldn't Medea grovel? All that is unnatural seems natural to him.

Well, he says. My sons shouldn't suffer because of their mother.

They leave in a kind of procession, led by Jason. Aeson and Promachus bearing the stone cups, careful and proud, two slaves holding the dress as if it were a body lying in the air, third slave holding the diadem outspread like wings. Funerary wedding procession.

Medea left alone. Another threshold crossed, as when she first aided Jason against the bulls or sliced her brother's throat. No part of Medea's life may be undone. Each action of hers remains forever. Pelias will not be made young. These cups of poison cannot mean nothing.

She fills a goatskin with water, wraps dates and bread in coarse linen. They will need enough food and water to reach

Athens, but they must also travel quickly. Only a few hours to get away from Korinth before Glauce and Kreon will begin to burn.

Medea will be dragging her sons. They won't want to go, won't understand. She'll have blood again on her hands from their wrists. She'll take the main path at first, to move quickly, and when she hears the cries from town, she'll lead her sons into wilderness, into this world too large where any may be lost. They'll follow the coast until they reach Aegeus. She'll offer him her younger body, bear new children for another king, enslaved again, but what other choice does she have? The kingdom of Medea is without subjects, without land, without reference.

Hekate guide me, Medea says. More powerful Nute. Shape some future I cannot see. Find some new kingdom, sever me from all that has come before. Let me rule and not be ruled.

A life of blood. No doubt she will need to kill Aegeus, too, or someone else in Athens, and more blood after. If she rules as king, it will be far away and many years from now. She understands that her kingdom will not be won easily, that all are against her. Women of Korinth. They watched and did nothing, so Medea would see them burn before she leaves, the entire city razed, all its brick soldiers, all its wealth and pride. The people of Iolcus, too, should have paid, and the stupid subjects of Cyzicus. She would be a wrath much larger. She would destroy all. And she wonders why this is. Rage, but others feel rage. The difference in her is that nothing will hold her back. She will do what is monstrous, because monstrous is only the absence of a lie, the great lie of what we are to each other, wife and husband, daughter and father, sister and brother, subject and king. In the absence of that lie, a great freedom, any action possible. She will feel nothing after the death of Glauce and Kreon. She could have eaten that stew of Pelias and the ram.

Her slaves return.

Where are my sons?

The oldest slave steps forward, head bowed. They're playing with the princess. We thought you'd be pleased. At first she wouldn't see them, but Jason made her come out, and then she was delighted.

You were supposed to return with my sons. What have you done?

The slave drops to her knees. I'm sorry. I didn't know. We thought this was what you wanted. She and the king have agreed to let your sons stay here in Korinth. This is what you wanted.

Medea slaps her as hard as she can. You stupid fool. Bring my sons back to me.

This woman shrinks away in pain and fear, worthless, mute.

Did they drink? Medea demands. Glauce and Kreon, did they drink from the cups?

Yes, the youngest slave says, stepping forward, shielding the woman Medea has slapped. A daughter defending her mother, Medea sees now. Your oldest gave cups to Kreon and Glauce, and the little one, Promachus, drank from his. Little face disappearing in honey and cinnamon, pouring all down the front of him. Everyone laughed. There's nothing better he could have done to make all love him.

And then they drank?

Yes, they drank the nectar. The king said it had something strange he'd never tasted before. The princess said it tasted like a flower, like a scent, a drink you could smell more than taste, and she kept drinking more, trying to find that scent and name it. And then she changed into the dress and diadem and looked so beautiful, so foreign, and all said so.

Was Jason delighted? Did he find her beautiful?

No answer to that. Only fear as the slaves watch Medea.

Bring my sons back now, Medea says. Hurry.

But we thought you wanted them to stay with the princess.

Medea strikes the younger slave now. Would any mother send her children away? And to her husband's new fuck? How stupid can you be? Bring them back now, or I slit your mother's throat with this knife.

But what can I tell the princess?

Tell her I want to say good-bye to my children. Then I'll be gone. All can forget me.

Too long waiting. Her sons not returned. Goatskin of water slung over her shoulder, and food for the journey to Athens, but time is what they need most. They must be outside the city before the poison begins to work.

Glauce spinning somewhere in her new dress, and Medea's children chasing the hem, laughing and running round and round in idiotic delight. She can see their open mouths, and Promachus tucking his neck, trying to be cute. Her three men all fighting for the love of young Glauce. Jason believing he will have all: kingdom, flesh, more sons.

So much poison, far more than needed. It will act soon. Glauce falling as she spins, clutching at her throat. Heavy golden sun around her neck, fire woven. She will say she's burning, and Jason will not see flame. The air without sign. Burning, she'll insist, as if fire could take new form. She'll reach for that funeral diadem of long golden petals, hammered suns, and her slaves won't know what to do. She'll want water, want to throw herself into a well, but the poison will bend her, drop her to the ground, deep cramp and pain, bound by golden rope. She'll turn to liquid, void her bowels and vomit and bleed and sweat, the dress no longer white or pure, and her father will rush to her, collapse over her body and the burning will engulf him too, rare contagion from air or wrath of gods without reason. Beautiful, innocent Glauce and her good father, mild Kreon, caught in some inferno without cause. But then they'll remember the drink, honey and cinnamon and something else, rare flower, and Medea hopes they have enough time before death to think of the first wife.

But her children still are not returned, young slave not believing what Medea will do. Her mother knelt on this floor and Medea's hand on the knife.

Where are my children! she demands. She can't be in this room any longer, rushes into the street and hears cries from the citadel. So it has begun. No time for escape. She won't leave without her children. Stone walls, city grown too large.

Aeson! she screams. Promachus! The women of Korinth watching her, hearing the cries from the citadel, guards watching also. All have stopped, a day that will never be forgotten. Shriek of a princess burning, voice of a terrified king too high, shouts of slaves helpless. Voices lost together. Medea the still point, center to which all are about to collapse.

The young slave running, a child herself pulling children. Medea watches her forever. Long hair swinging side to side, feet high over the stones and seeming never to touch, sun and shadow in flashes until it's unclear which is absence, and she never comes closer. Medea's sons stumbling behind, yanked by their thin arms, and unmoving. Guards beyond, shafts of spears and dull bronze, shields turning in some breeze like leaves. World bursting, made too full, too much weight for any surface to hold. Medea sinking into stone.

Sound rising behind her. More spears and shields, but she cannot turn to look, can only wait for her sons. So small and unlikely, pulled through air in odd twists as if they might fly if not caught by an arm, insubstantial, bodies not held to the earth. Grotesque faces of giants at their backs, gaining, reaching, faces carved by helmets into slats and mouths bare and animal.

My children, Medea says, and is able to raise her hand through air too heavy, meets them as they collide against her, bodies too soft, hearts beating, heat and sweat and scent and crying, frightened.

Spears from every side, air lanced by shaft and point. She hugs her sons close, would pull them inside her ribs, but she is too soft and they are too soft. They will be skewered and held aloft, her babies. My children, she says. Every spear arm pulled back, ready now to thrust, the circle closing, world of men.

Medea's hand on Aeson's cheek. She lifts his chin, pulls him against her breast, hugs him tight as she slices her knife across his throat.

Hot blood on her hands, Aeson jerking against her side. She presses her forehead to his, looks into the last of his eyes, her baby. Panic and pain. Don't be afraid, she says. Feels his body slack, blood slowing, no longer pouring out, no longer fighting, calming, and she must let him fall away from her. From breast onto stone, body unstrung, lying on his side so peacefully in deep red blood, a color so rich in this light, without shadow.

She holds Promachus now, who is crying and struggling, but she lifts his face to hers, kisses him as the blade cuts through, holds him tight to let him know he is not alone, is loved, puts her cheek against his for last warmth. His hands scratching at her, punching her, but she clings to him, keeps him safe.

My children, she says. My babies. She keeps Promachus pressed close, reaches down for Aeson, holds both, her face in their hair, breathing them. She would stay like this forever now. There is nothing left, nowhere else to go. Nute, she says. Bring night, endless night. Let there never be day again. Swallow this world.

But the guards come closer. Not enough for them, not enough what she has lost. Animals! she screams. She pulls back Aeson's head, fills her mouth with blood from his throat, spits it at the guards. Let them be covered in her children's blood.

They step back, and she drinks again, lurches forward and sprays the air to turn it dark. Bright air black.

They fall away, these coward men, retreat with their spears. Medea, broken king, dragging her sons over the earth, one in each fist, mouth painted with their blood. Form of fear, earth god unnamed. Jason won't dare follow. None will follow. Beyond human law, at war with the sun.

Acknowledgments

I first read *Medea* when I was an undergraduate at Stanford, in a year-long Great Works of Western Literature course (the final year it was offered). The instructor, Leslie Cahoon, was a classicist and feminist who shaped nearly all my future interests. Because of her I took a feminist thought workshop with Adrienne Rich, learned Latin and am currently translating Ovid, studied all of Chaucer's works in graduate school, learned Old English and translated *Beowulf*, became interested in depictions of hell from Bede to Dante to Blake to McCarthy, and of course became influenced by the Greeks. My novels are all Greek tragedies, I'm a neoclassical writer, and it was a particular pleasure to try to bring Medea more fully to life after twenty-five years of thinking about her. So I want to thank Leslie for her enormous and lasting influence.

I thank you to archaeologist Cheryl Ward for inviting me to help build and then captain the reconstruction of one of Hatshepsut's ships from 3,500 years ago. She was the one who held the project together, and that rich experience is the basis for all the descriptions of the Argo here.

I also want to thank John L'Heureux, as always, for more than twenty years of mentorship and for his sharp early read.

Huge thanks to Elisabeth Schmitz and Katie Raissian and others at Grove for having faith in this novel, which had been previously delayed. It was written four years ago and should have followed *Goat Mountain* as the culmination in style and content of a set of Greek tragedies about religion, so I'm very happy it can finally have a life.

And I'd like to thank my fabulous agents Kim Witherspoon, David Forrer, and Lyndsey Blessing at Inkwell and Rob Kraitt at Casarotto. Also Robin Robertson for his new and excellent translation of *Medea* from which I drew the title.